"What a little thing you are," he murmured

"My hands could almost meet around you." His hands enclosed Gemma's waist, drawing her back against him. It seemed absolutely natural that she should lean back. It was as if she'd done it a hundred times before.

"Not so very little," she laughed shakily. "Look, my head reaches up way beyond your shoulder." Keep it light, she thought desperately.

"So it does," Harn said. "Just the right height for me." He rubbed his mouth against her hair.

This was fooling, of course, Gemma reminded herself, just the merest of flirtations. Perhaps not routine behavior with his secretary, but then their relationship had been somewhat out of the ordinary right from the start.

Her head was lowered. Turning her around, he tipped her chin up with his forefinger. She knew he was going to kiss her, and the urgency of her need for it to happen was almost shocking....

Books by Marjorie Lewty

HARLEQUIN ROMANCES

HARLEQUIN PRESENTS

These books may be available at your local bookseller.

For a free catalog listing all titles currently available, send your name and address to:

Harlequin Reader Service
2504 West Southern Avenue, Tempe, AZ 85282
Canadian address: Stratford, Ontario N5A 6W2

Dangerous Male

Marjorie Lewty

Harlequin Books

TORONTO • NEW YORK • LONDON
AMSTERDAM • PARIS • SYDNEY • HAMBURG
STOCKHOLM • ATHENS • TOKYO • MILAN

Original hardcover edition published in 1983
by Mills & Boon Limited

ISBN 0-373-02587-4

Harlequin Romance first edition December 1983

CHAPTER ONE

BETH was right, the man was an inhuman bastard. Gemma Lawson fought down a surge of anger and disgust as she met the cold grey eyes that regarded her from the opposite side of the large mahogany desk. Not that Beth had used that particular word. 'Inhuman beast' was the way she had put it. Beth's generation wasn't as forthright with its language as her young stepsister Gemma's was.

Harn Durrant's shoulders moved impatiently under their immaculately-tailored lightweight suiting. 'So you see, Miss—er——' he glanced down at the pad on which he had jotted Gemma's name when she walked unceremoniously into his office five minutes ago '—Miss Lawson, I'm afraid you're wasting your time. And mine,' he added, with a pointed look towards the door.

Gemma's eyes were as deep blue as the ocean and could look as cold. At this moment they looked arctic. 'You mean you're prepred to throw my sister out, just like that, when she's worked for the firm for seventeen years, ever since she was seventeen? When she's been your father's trusted and confidential secretary for ten of those years?'

The grey eyes looked up at the ceiling as if seeking patience. 'That's just the point, I'm afraid, Miss Lawson. Your sister has been in one job too long, she's got into a rut and she can't get out of it. Things move on, you know. This will soon be a very different firm from the one that my father managed for most of his life.' His glance flicked with distaste round the shabby office with its old-fashioned office furniture, its metal filing cabinet, its cracking ceiling with the yellowing stucco frieze. 'It suited him as it was, but it certainly doesn't suit me.' Strong brown fingers closed over the worn leather arms of the director's chair as if they would mould them to his will. 'I intend to transform this firm so that it's ready to crash into the twenty-first century.'

Yes, thought Gemma, looking with dislike at the dark, lean face, the deep-set grey eyes with the strange, darker rims round the irises, the hard mouth. Yes, 'crash' would be the right word. Everything this man did would be violent. Even his name—Harn Durrant—sounded savage, ruthless.

'At least,' she said, 'you could have given Beth time to adapt. She hasn't——'

'Time!' he barked. 'How much longer does she need? She's had five training sessions on the word-processor, which is more than is considered necessary for a competent secretary. She's moaned and groaned about it, never really concentrated.' His lips curled. 'And yesterday she even had the nerve to tell me that she intended to go on using the old Remington typewriter that should have been pensioned off years ago—that she wasn't prepared to learn the new technology. No, it's quite obvious that your sister isn't up to the job, and anyone who isn't willing to change isn't going to remain in this company very long now I'm in charge. I don't have any room for passengers.' The grey eyes moved away from her without interest. 'And now, Miss Lawson, I'm very busy. I've allowed you to come in here without an interview and interrupt me at my work. In view of the fact that your sister was my father's secretary I've taken the time to explain matters to you in some detail, but my time is valuable and I can't spare any more of it. I must ask you to leave.'

'No,' said Gemma. 'Not yet.'

His head shot up. 'What did you say?'

'I said no,' Gemma repeated firmly. 'I've listened to your utterly contemptible statement and I'm not going until you hear what I have to say.' She stood up, because it was going to be easier to say what she had to say standing on her own two feet.

Harn Durrant scowled up at her darkly. 'I've no intention of——' he began angrily, but she interrupted him just as he had interrupted her a few moments before.

'You'll jolly well listen, Mr Durrant—unless you're prepared to have me thrown out. And I doubt if old Ted would consent to throw me out, even if you ordered him to. He's a good friend of mine, I've known him since I was a little girl.'

Harn Durrant sat back in his chair. His eyes moved slowly from the smooth wheat-fair hair, held by a black velvet ribbon, to the small, pretty breasts which were at the moment heaving up and down slightly with nerves and anger under a white silky blouse. Gemma felt a flush rise to her cheeks. She was quite accustomed to being looked at by men—she was young and pretty and desirable— but there was something about this particular man that sent shock-waves passing through her.

At last he spoke. 'Well, say what you have to say, but make it brief.'

'I will,' said Gemma. 'I'm just as anxious to

dispense with your company, Mr Durrant, as you are with mine. What I have to say is this. My sister has only just got over a bad attack of 'flu. She's had no chance of getting back into working routine gently—you saw to that, didn't you? You worked her until eight o'clock and after every day she got home tired out—so tired that she was unable to sleep. She hasn't been in any state to cope with anything new, but did you make allowance for that? No, you thrust her head-first into this micro-chip thing, and when she couldn't grasp it straight away you——' she wrinkled her short, straight little nose contemptuously '—I think "dispensed with her services" was the tactful way you put it, wasn't it, Mr Durrant?'

Gemma had come here with a vague idea of making this man change his mind, but now she had seen him she knew beyond doubt that he wouldn't. She also knew that darling Beth would never be even moderately happy working for him. Beth was warm and loving and sensitive. She had been almost like a daughter to old Mr Durrant and hadn't yet got over his death, two months ago. She certainly wasn't in any state to cope with a man like his son, Harn Durrant, a man who would drain away any girl's confidence with that contemptuous look of his, and Gemma decided there and then that her sister wasn't going to come back to work out her month's notice. Somehow she, Gemma, would get a job and begin to pull her weight so that Beth could take it easy for a while and not have the whole burden of keeping the home going for the two of them.

'Yes, I believe that was the way I put it,' Harn Durrant said coolly. 'I also remember that I arranged for a very handsome hand-out for her—much in excess of what was required. It could almost be termed a golden handshake, in fact.'

'Money!' Gemma tossed her head in fine contempt, and her mane of fair hair slapped against her neck. 'Money doesn't make up for the insulting way you rejected her! If your father had known——'

The grey eyes narrowed. 'I think I've taken quite enough from you, Miss Lawson. I don't know why you came here in the first place, and you certainly haven't made me disposed to change my mind. If it's any satisfaction to you, you may tell your sister that I'm sorry she feels she has been treated less than fairly, but I can't reconsider my decision. This affair has been extremely inconvenient for me. I'm going to London for a few days next week and I had hoped that by now your sister would have adapted to my way of work so that I could leave her in charge of the office. Instead of which she proved herself completely incapable of coping.' He laughed nastily. 'Women—you're all the same! You say you want equality, and then when you're faced with a challenge you go to pieces.'

Gemma couldn't let that go. Anger overcame the nervousness she had felt at first when confronted with this formidable individual who held her sister's future in his relentless hands. 'How dare you say that!' she blazed. 'If anybody can rise to a challenge my sister Beth can. I don't suppose you would know what it's like to be left alone at seventeen, with very little money and a year-old baby sister to look after? You wouldn't know, would you, Mr Durrant? You've always had money, position, haven't you?' The words tumbled out, almost of their own accord as she warmed to her subject. 'Well, that was a challenge if you like—twice as daunting as—as learning to work some silly word-processing machine. Beth could have opted out—she could have put me into a home—after all, she isn't any blood relative, I'm only her stepsister. But she didn't. She rose to the challenge. She gave up her plans to go to art school. She worked at nights to learn shorthand and typing. She got a job in this company and over the years she rose to be your father's trusted secretary. She's been wonderful to me, all my life, she's a grand person. But you wouldn't appreciate qualities like that, would you, Mr Durrant? All you want is a super-girl with more head than heart, who can work your marvellous new technology for you. Well, I hope you find her, and good luck to both of you! Certainly I don't envy any girl who works for you.'

She turned to the door. 'Thank you for listening,' she said. Her knees were trembling now, all she wanted was to get away as quickly as possible. 'Good morning, Mr Durrant.'

'Wait a minute,' he rapped out, getting to his feet. Standing, he was even more formidable. He must have been well over six feet, with the broad shoulders and slim hips of an athlete. He walked slowly round the desk and stood towering over Gemma. A shiver passed through her as she felt the impact of his devastating masculinity. Beth had said he was a womaniser. 'Girls hanging round him by the minute,' she'd told Gemma with a scornful twist of her mouth. 'I just hate working for that sort of man. Not that he'd look twice at me,' she had added with a wry laugh.

'Come back and sit down again,' he said now to Gemma, and she felt herself bristle at his dictatorial tone. He was a perfect illustration of the term 'male chauvinist'. 'There's something more to be said.'

'Not by me,' she said shortly. She needed to get away from this man, who was having an unnerving effect on her. And she wanted to get back to Beth, who had been in a dreadful state when Gemma left the house earlier this morning.

'No, by me,' he put in smoothly. 'Come along, don't be touchy just because I happen to have told you the truth about a few things.' He gripped her wrist and she found herself being helplessly impelled towards the chair she had just vacated. She sat there dithering with fury while he went round and seated himself opposite once again. How dared he—how *dared* he put his hands on her! Her wrist was tingling where his fingers had touched it. She would have got up and run out of the office, only she was afraid that her legs wouldn't carry her to the door.

He leaned back in the worn leather chair and surveyed her in silence for so long that she felt like screaming. Then he said calmly, 'And what do *you* do for a living, Miss Lawson?'

She glared back at him. 'Does that really concern you?'

He pursed his lips thoughtfully. 'I don't know yet. It well might. Do you have any objection to telling me?'

'All right, as you're so interested in me, I'm a typist.'

'H'm.' A gleam that might have been amusement touched the cold grey eyes. 'Not a secretary? Most typists call themselves secretaries these days, I find.'

'I'm a typist,' Gemma repeated firmly. She wasn't even a typist, actually, she hadn't yet quite finished her course at the secretarial college, but she wasn't going to tell this horrible man *that*.

'And you have a job?'

'I'm between jobs at present,' she improvised airily. 'I have one or two offers, but I haven't decided yet which to accept. Now, if you'll excuse me, Mr Durrant——' She put one hand on the desk to help to lever herself up, as her knees still felt distinctly odd.

'Oh, for Pete's sake, girl, sit down and don't jump about like a puppet on a string!' he burst out irritably. 'That's what I want to talk to you about. If your sister is unwell, as you tell me, and not able to come to the office to work out her notice, I need to engage someone else. You strike me as a tolerably bright girl, and if you can spell, and type reasonably well, you might fill the bill and save me interviewing a string of probably hopeless applicants. In London I should have no trouble, but this town does not, I imagine, produce the cream of the secretarial market.' He smiled sourly. 'And as you may have gathered already, Miss Lawson, I'm not an easy man to work for. I don't tolerate fools gladly. I may be wrong, but I don't think you're a fool. And you would at least start out with no false ideas about me.'

Gemma's blue eyes widened in horror. Work for this hateful—overbearing—unfeeling—*brute*? She'd rather join the queue at the unemployment office! Which was probably just what she would be doing when she finished her course in July. Jobs were not so easy to come by, she knew that, and particularly if you had no previous experience. A picture of the rates demand form—and the gas bill—and the electricity bill—appeared again before her eyes. Beth's redundancy payment would cover them, of course, but how much better if she could keep the money, however much it was, to set herself up in something new—something she would enjoy.

Harn Durrant was watching her face closely. 'Your last job—shorthand and typing, was it?'

'Audio-typing,' Gemma said. 'Most men, I find, prefer to use a dictating machine these days. It's so much quicker and more convenient.' She was quoting shamelessly from her tutor at college, who had advanced ideas. Most of the girls took shorthand courses, but Gemma had wanted to qualify in the shortest possible time and she had opted to concentrate on her typing.

Harn Durrant seemed to approve of that. 'No problem, then. I prefer to use tape myself.' Again that sour smile. 'I haven't the time to spend admiring a girl's legs while she takes down my immortal words in shorthand.' He tapped his gold Biro on the desk and said briskly, 'Well then, Miss Lawson, what about it? Shall we give it a try for, say, one month?'

Everything in Gemma wanted to yell, 'No—no—not in a million years would I work for you!' That would have been the most sensible thing to do. And yet—and yet—there was something about the man sitting on the other side of the desk, observing her with those strange grey eyes, that made her want to accept the challenge. She'd like to—to *show* him. What she wanted to show him she wasn't quite sure. Perhaps, she thought, it was her ridiculous compulsion to take up a challenge. It had got her into trouble before—even at school it was generally known that Gemma Lawson could be relied on to accept a dare. She should be forewarned now.

But she heard herself say, 'But you don't know anything about me, Mr Durrant. Wouldn't you want to take up references?' That would finish it, of course, because there weren't any references. There hadn't been any job. In fact, she had blithely concocted a lot of lies.

He shook his head. 'Waste of time,' he said in a clipped voice. 'I don't rely on other people's opinions, I make up my own mind. But as a matter of interest, perhaps you will tell me why you left your last job.'

It was horrid—one lie leads to another inevitably. 'I—I wanted to better my prospects,' she said. 'I wanted to be free to look for something more interesting.'

He looked keenly at her for so long that she began to feel hollow inside. It was as if he could read her mind. But when he spoke he merely said, 'You consider yourself ambitious?'

'Oh *yes*!' That was the truth at least. She *was* ambitious—partly for her own sake but even more for Beth's. She wanted to be able to repay Beth for all she had sacrificed over the years. Beth had given her everything, all through her childhood and schooldays. Everything—and love as well. Or perhaps principally love. Warmth ran through her as she thought of all Beth had done for her. Now, for the first time, Beth needed *her* help and she would do anything—anything, to ease the strain for her stepsister. That rates demand——

'What would you be willing to pay me?' She met the grey eyes squarely.

He looked amused. 'That's what I like to hear— a girl who isn't afraid to ask. You could hardly expect to start on the same salary that your sister has been getting, of course, but I would say—let me see——' He looked out of the window and then back at her, naming a sum that had Gemma blinking, while trying not to show her surprise. 'That, I think, is quite a good offer, Miss Lawson, as I would be taking you on trust. Of course, your salary would go up rapidly if you proved your worth to me. I take it you don't share your sister's horror of technology and would be willing to train on the word-processor?'

'I—I——' Gemma swallowed. Everything was moving far too quickly. She felt as if she had walked into a trap. Then, 'Yes,' she said firmly, 'I should be very interested in learning.' Her spirits began to rise. There were electric typewriters at the secretarial college, but nothing more ambitious. But if she could get a training here on a word-processor, if she could start her working life with the most up-to-date qualifications, there would be no limit to the kind of job she could eventually land. Perhaps she could even take over the whole responsibility for the house and free Beth at last to take up her beloved art.

For this chance she would even brave the prospect of working for the intimidating Harn Durrant for a short time. It would be bound to be very short, she thought wryly, she didn't think she could stand him for long.

'Then that's arranged,' he said crisply. 'You can start tomorrow—nine o'clock sharp.'

A couple of minutes later Gemma found herself outside in the street. The premises of Durrants (Fine Paper) Limited were in an old building in a side street of the middle-sized Midlands town, a few minutes' walk from a pleasant park. Gemma made her way here now and sat down on a seat, in the shade of a flowering cherry tree, to recover.

What had she done? Twenty minutes ago she had entered Durrants' office, smiling her sweetest smile at Ted Baines, who served in the shop downstairs, where stacks of paper reposed on every shelf, and in the tiers of drawers which reached to the ceiling and overflowed into folders on the wide wooden counter.

Ted had beamed at Gemma; he was always delighted to see her. Ted was knocking sixty now and had worked at Durrants since he was a lad. Ever since Beth had come to work here, and brought her little stepsister into the shop sometimes, he had watched Gemma grow from a pretty toddler, to a long-legged schoolchild, to the lovely young girl she was now—slim and straight, with candid, long-lashed blue eyes in a small, piquante face that could twist suddenly with humour, or soften with compassion.

''Morning, Miss Gemma. You looking for your sister? She's not in today.'

'No, I know, Ted, I've left her at home. She's not feeling too good—hasn't really got over that dose of 'flu.'

Not feeling too good was an understatement. As

she smiled at Ted Gemma remembered, with a pang, how Beth had lain on her back with the bedclothes pulled up nearly covering her face. How she had looked frighteningly blank when she had muttered that she wasn't going in to the office today; how she had turned away from Gemma when she asked what was wrong, and should she get the doctor. She had shaken her head and said she wasn't ill. 'I can't go,' she had repeated. 'I can't. I can't.' And she had begun to weep silently, helplessly.

Nerves, Gemma had thought. She's been working up for this ever since the new man took over. And yesterday there had been some sort of unpleasantness between them. Beth had come in looking terrible, but wouldn't say much about it to Gemma, except that Mr Durrant wanted her to work on a new electronic machine that she hated the very sight of. And now—this!

It was more than just nerves, Gemma thought with cold fear trickling down her back. A nervous breakdown? Oh heavens, what should she do? She had stroked Beth's dark hair and soothed her. 'Never mind, darling, you don't have to go if you don't want to. I'll let them know. Now, you take a couple of aspirins and have a good sleep. And don't *worry*—I'll look after everything.'

It was up to her now, she was on her own. All these years Beth had coped and now she'd reached the end. Losing her job had defeated her finally.

Ted had stroked his thinning fair hair back, looked over his spectacles and said, 'There now, I'm not surprised—she's not looked herself lately. Ever since old Mr Durrant went.' He sighed and clicked his tongue. 'It's made a difference to all of us, that it has. Working for the young one isn't the same at all.'

'Is he here, Ted?' Gemma had asked, although she knew he was—she had spotted his gleaming dark green Mercedes in the small car-park at the side of the building. 'Can I go up? I want to have a word with him.'

Ted had lifted the counter partition on its hinges. 'Yes, of course, you go up, Miss Gemma.' And as she walked through the shop and up the creaking wooden staircase he had murmured something that sounded like, 'And don't you take any nonsense from him.'

Well, she hadn't. Or had she? She sat on the park seat now, wondering, trying to remember exactly how she had got herself into this position, but all she could think of was Harn Durrant's strange grey eyes, with the darker rim round the irises, holding her own as he regarded her across the desk. Those eyes had an almost hypnotic quality about them, she thought, shivering slightly, although the late spring day was warm.

Why had he offered her the job?—that was the question. Gemma pondered this for some time, and two possible answers finally suggested themselves. The first was that she was young and presumably anxious to get ahead and learn all the new technology that had baffled and upset Beth. He would bank on training—or bullying—her into his own ways. The second was that he might, in some part, assuage a bad conscience by employing the sister of the old and trusted employee he had so ruthlessly dismissed. The third possibility, which didn't even occur to her, was that something about her might have impressed him. On the whole she favoured the first answer. Harn Durrant didn't strike her as a man who would be much troubled by conscience. Business first, human being a long way after—that would be his working plan.

Well, if he was making a convenience of her she would have no qualms about doing the same to him. She would take on the job, draw the very handsome salary he had offered her for one month, learn everything she could in that space of time, and then hand in her notice. If, by then, she had succeeded in making herself useful to him, so much the better. He would be paid back in his own coin. Meanwhile she would put up with his nasty ways for the sake of the business experience and so that they could pay the rates without having to use Beth's redundancy money.

Having come to this conclusion, Gemma felt slightly better about everything. The worst, however, was yet to come, and she had a horrible sinking feeling in her stomach when she thought of it. She had to go home and face Beth with the news.

'Gemma love, you can't! You simply *can't*, I won't let you.' Beth sat back in the old basket chair with the faded cushion and stared at her young stepsister in dismay.

'I can and I will,' Gemma smiled. She was so relieved to find Beth up, and not lying in bed having a nervous breakdown, that she could almost treat the whole interview with Harn Durrant as a kind of black joke. Beth looked very pale and there were deep rings under her soft brown eyes, but her wavy dark hair was carefully drawn back into its usual knot at the back of her neck and her sensitive mouth was firm and composed. Beth, Gemma realised, had been making a tremendous effort during her absence.

She leaned forward now and put a hand on Gemma's arm. 'I'm sorry I was so wet this morning, Gem,' she said ruefully. 'I don't know what came over me. Of course I'll go back and work out my notice—I'll go back tomorrow. Meanwhile I'll look for another job. That so-and-so Harn Durrant won't refuse to give me a reference, I shouldn't think, even if it *isn't* as a word-processor expert. Then you can go on and take your exams and look for a job yourself—a nice job that you'll enjoy. Not working for a man like *him*. Good gracious, fancy making your entry into the business world in a slave job like that would be—no, I won't allow it.'

Gemma's blue eyes were dancing. 'You can't stop it, Sis. I'm eighteen now, remember? If I want to sell my freedom for filthy lucre, slaving for a harsh master, then I shall do so.' She squeezed Beth's hand tightly. 'Now don't worry about me, I'm tough, and no Harn Durrant will intimidate me. And you know, I don't mind the idea of learning this technology thing that you hate so much. I was quite good at maths at school. Miss Webster even admitted that I might have a logical mind—think of that! I rather fancy becoming a word-processor wizard and commanding a top job, with salary to match. Now, let's discuss what you're going to do with your redundancy money. I think you should go to art school—you'd get in as a "mature student"——' she pulled a face '—that sounds silly, looking at you. You look so young, Sis.'

She was watching Beth's face closely and she saw the look of longing that passed over it, like the sun coming through dark clouds. Then it was gone again. 'Oh, I couldn't, it's too late.' She shook her head. 'I must get another job, I can't start being a student now, love, it's too absurd.'

'It isn't absurd at all,' Gemma said stoutly. 'Anyway, think about it, and don't toss the idea out straight away. You might get a grant and that would help, and if I'm earning, we could manage fine.'

She almost said, 'You and Ian could get married,' but stopped herself in time. She was quite sure that Ian Jackson was in love with Beth—had been for more than two years, but Beth would never admit that he was anything more than a friend. He was an artist, lived in a bedsitter at the bottom end of the town, and he and Beth had met two years ago when he had come into Durrants to enquire about some special water-colour paper he needed. They had struck up a friendship immediately. To Beth it was wonderful to know a real artist, to be able to meet and talk about art—which they did frequently. Ian had formed the habit of coming to supper every Saturday evening, and Gemma couldn't miss the way Beth took on a new sparkle when he was there.

'I like Ian, I think he's a pet. Why don't you two get married?' Gemma had enquired at the beginning, with the straight-to-the-point ingenuousness of a sixteen-year-old.

Beth had gone pink and laughed it off with the remark that chance would be a fine thing, but Gemma had realised, as the months went by and she grew in understanding, that Ian was the kind of dedicated artist who wasn't likely to make much money. 'I can only get rich by being a bad artist,' he had grinned ruefully once, in her presence, 'and that doesn't appeal.'

So Ian had gone on coming to supper on Saturday evenings, and sometimes Beth would visit him in his studio-bedsitter and come back with a funny, depressed look on her lovely face, and Gemma knew that she was wishing there was some way for the two of them to be together. But Ian had very little money and he wouldn't compromise his art. Beth had a house to keep going and a younger sister to put through her training. It all seemed hopeless.

Beth was sitting very quietly now and her brown eyes were cloudy. 'No,' she said again, 'it's much too late for me to think of going to art school, it wouldn't do at all. Anyway, love, you'll never stick working for that awful Harn Durrant for more than a month.'

That was Gemma's opinion too, but she didn't admit it. She jumped up and made for the kitchen. 'Let's have some coffee,' she said gaily, 'and you can instruct me in the office work at Durrant's, because I fully intend to turn up there tomorrow morning and confront Mr Harn Durrant with the consequences of his rash decision to employ me.'

In the small kitchen she spooned instant coffee into two mugs and waited for the kettle to boil. Her announcement had passed off better than she could have expected. She had been able to make a big joke of it and Beth, she was sure, wouldn't object too strongly when she left tomorrow morning. Gemma had seen the relief on her stepsister's face when she realised that she wasn't going to have to make the tremendous effort herself.

This time the effort would come from Gemma. It was up to her now, and she mustn't fail.

Confidence, that's all I need, she told herself, But the sinking feeling in the pit of her stomach reminded her that what she had undertaken was no joke. No joke at all, she thought, as the dark, hard face of Harn Durrant appeared before her mind's eye and she heard again that smooth, deep, almost menacing voice say, 'I'm not an easy man to work for, Miss Lawson, and I don't tolerate fools gladly.'

Oh lordy, thought Gemma bleakly, what have I let myself in for?

Nine o'clock sharp, the man had said, and Gemma was in the office at two minutes to nine, but Harn Durrant was already at his desk when she presented herself, her heart beating very fast.

His dark head was bent over a sheaf of documents and he didn't lift it as Gemma went in. She stood beside the desk and waited for him to notice her presence, which, eventually, he did. He lifted his head and again she felt the impact of those strange grey eyes under their long black lashes. His lashes were, Gemma remarked, unfairly thick and silky for a man, and they curved outwards at the corners so that they gave the impression of a faint smile. Which, Gemma was to discover, was altogether misleading. Harn Durrant smiled very seldom, and he certainly wasn't smiling now.

'What do you——' he began irritably, and then, 'Oh lord, yes, you're the new girl. Well, have you

fixed things up with Mrs Blake? Insurance cards
and so on?'

Gemma's heart missed a beat. Why hadn't she
thought of that? And why hadn't Beth? But of
course, she hadn't confessed to Beth that she had
misled Harn Durrant about her lack of experience,
and now she was going to be found out in a lie on
her very first morning.

'Er—no,' she said, and then, brightly, 'I thought
I would come up here to you first, Mr Durrant, to
see if there was anything urgent you wanted me to
do.'

He gave her a withering look. 'I can't use your
services until you're on the staff. Go along and see
Mrs Brown. She knows that your sister's leaving,
of course, but I haven't told her anything further.
You can do the explaining.'

'Yes, sir,' said Gemma obediently, turning to the
door.

'And Miss Lawson——' the peremptory voice
stopped her, 'I dislike being called sir—by women,
that is. You will call me Mr Durrant, and I shall
call you—what is your name, by the way?'

'Gemma,' she told him, and saw him jot the
word down on a writing pad. Goodness, she *had*
made an impression on him, hadn't she? He
couldn't even be sure of remembering her name.

'Very well, Gemma, go along now, and then
come back here as quickly as you can.' And that's
an order, he seemed to be adding silently.

'Yes, s—— Mr Durrant,' said Gemma. She
closed the door quietly behind her and pulled a
face at it from the outside.

The general office was on the ground floor,
behind the shop, and Mrs Brown was in charge

here. She was a middle-aged woman with untidy grey hair and a cheerful smile. So far as Gemma knew, from Beth, this lady somehow managed to cope with all the work of the office that wasn't directly in the managing director's province, with the assistance of a young typist and an office girl who took messages, went to the post, and did all the odd jobs, including making several brews of tea in the course of the day. Mrs Brown had worked for old Mr Durrant for many years and had already been a fixture when Beth joined the staff. 'Mrs Brown can't get along without her cup of tea,' Beth had once told Gemma, with a twinkle in her soft brown eyes. 'And she certainly earns it.'

Mrs Brown looked up from a vast rolltop desk littered with forms and papers and gave Gemma a look that would have been approriate for a funeral. 'Oh, Gemma, I am so sorry, it's upset me terribly—about Beth, I mean. When Mr Durrant told me she was leaving us I couldn't believe it— the office won't be the same without her. I've thought she hasn't been looking at all well lately, and that last bout of 'flu must have pulled her down terribly. Tell me, how is she? What does the doctor say? Is it something really serious?'

Gemma felt a sense of relief. At least the Durrant man had had the decency not to broadcast the reason for Beth's dismissal. Mrs Brown evidently thought she had resigned for health reasons. 'Not really serious, so far as we know, but she has to have a long rest and take things very easily.'

Mrs Brown nodded sympathetically. 'And then she'll be coming back, do you think?'

Gemma shook her head. 'It's very doubtful,' she

said. 'Meanwhile,' she added brightly, 'Mr Durrant
has asked me to stand in for her—just on trial, of
course, to see how I get on. I've started this
morning and he sent me down to you to see about
insurance cards and so on, and put me on the staff
register.'

Mrs Brown's brow creased into a frown. 'But I
thought—Beth said you hadn't finished your
course yet, that you had still to take your exams.'

'I'll have to put them off,' said Gemma. 'I
thought this offer was too good to refuse.' She
crossed her fingers behind her back. 'It's all been a
bit sudden, Mrs Brown, and you see I don't know
about cards and so on. I was wondering if you'd
be good enough to help me.'

The frown disappeared. 'Of course I will, my
dear, and good luck to you.' She hesitated and
then pulled a wry face. 'You may find Mr Durrant
not too easy to work for. He's very different from
his father—full of up-to-date ideas, like most
young men. But you may get along very well with
him. You're young yourself and I know from Beth
that you're very bright.'

Gemma flushed. 'I just hope I'll be bright
enough, Mrs Brown. I'm going to try my best.
Er—perhaps I ought to tell you that Mr Durrant
got the impression that I'd been in a job before.
He didn't seem to want to know anything about it,
so I didn't tell him that I hadn't. He—sort of—
rushed me, if you know what I mean.'

Mrs Brown's mouth turned down at the corners.
'Indeed I know what you mean, Gemma. He's a
rusher all right, is our Mr Durrant. Don't let that
worry you, my dear, so long as you can do the job
that's all he's interested in. He's not one to be

impressed by bits of paper—although paper's our line, isn't it?' She laughed heartily at her own little joke. 'Now, go along up to him, my dear, and leave all the details to me. Call in and see me at lunch time and I'll have the forms ready for you to sign.'

Gemma thanked her and breathed a sigh of relief as she hurried up the creaking wooden staircase. That seemed to be the first hurdle crossed, but ahead of her was the real test.

As she reached the massive door of the managing director's office her mouth was dry and she had a sick, empty feeling inside. Not for the first time in her young life she wished she hadn't been born with this suicidal need to accept a challenge. This time, she thought, her hands clammy as they turned the door-handle, she had almost certainly bitten off more than she could chew.

CHAPTER TWO

HARN DURRANT wasn't sitting behind his desk as Gemma went in, he was riffling irritably through the drawers of a grey metal filing cabinet. He turned as she opened the door and gave her a long, assessing look, from the top of her smooth fair head to her black patent sandals and back again. Gemma was wearing the suit she had bought a few weeks ago, specially with an eye to interviews for a job, once her exams were over. It was inexpensive

but neat, and—she considered—suitable for the
purpose. A charcoal grey skirt, flaring slightly
from the hips, topped by a silky white blouse
with a thin black stripe and a demure collar. A
wide patent-leather belt hugged her slim waist.
She had brushed her wheat-fair hair until it
shone like satin and tied it back with a velvet
ribbon. Her skin was clear and soft and needed
no make-up except a touch of eye-shadow and a
light gloss on her lips.

She had got up early this morning and spent a
good deal of time making sure that her appearance,
at least, wouldn't let her down, however she might
perform as a secretary, and she met Harn
Durrant's critical gaze without flinching. But she
couldn't tell from his expression whether he was
satisfied or not, he merely removed his gaze to the
row of dog-eared folders in the drawer and
grunted, 'What a mess! This is the sort of outdated
system I mean to dispense with.' He pushed the
drawer and it closed with a clang, then drifted
open again.

He strode back to his desk and threw himself
into his chair. 'Now then, Gemma, to work. Your
desk's over there.' He gestured towards the far end
of the long room. 'My father liked to have his
secretary working in the same office with him, but
I have other ideas. However, this set-up here isn't
going to last long, so we may as well struggle on
with it for the moment. You'll find a couple of
cassettes ready to transcribe in the top drawer. I
like my letters with two copies—that is, until you
get the word-processor going, after which they'll
be stored on disc and no copies will be required.
I've arranged for your training to begin next

Monday, when I shall be away. Meanwhile you can, I take it, use an electronic typewriter?'

All this was delivered in a quick, almost aggressive tone, and Gemma felt quite stunned when he had finished. An electronic typewriter? Was that very different from the electric one she had been using at the secretarial school? She walked down the office to the typing desk. Here stood the space-age contraption that Beth had developed such a phobia about. There seemed to be two parts to it: on one side what she took to be the word-processor, with a small display screen, the size of a portable TV set, standing on top of it. On the other side was a typewriter—or what Gemma thought of as a typewriter with frills on, in the shape of rows of extra keys to right and left of the ordinary keyboard, marked with mysterious letters and symbols. Harn Durrant had followed her and was standing close behind, so close that Gemma felt vastly uncomfortable, and would have moved away except that she was hemmed in by the typing desk.

'Well?' he shot out.

The nearness of the man, the feeling of masculine strength and solidity that he seemed to radiate, was constricting her breathing. She swallowed with difficulty. 'I—I haven't used this particular model,' she said, indicating the typewriter part of the outfit, 'but I'm sure I can get the hang of it fairly soon. Is there an operator's guide?'

He began to pull out the drawers in the typing desk. 'Should be. That is, if your sister didn't tear it up in a rage.'

Gemma had made a firm resolution to keep her

cool and not let the man's sarcasm provoke her, but this was too much. 'That's a rotten thing to say!' she burst out hotly. 'As if Beth would do a thing like that!' She glared at him in dislike.

To her annoyance he smiled. Or perhaps it wasn't exactly a smile, it was just those curving eyelashes giving the impression of a smile. He folded his arms, leaning back against the filing cabinet and said, 'I wouldn't put it past her. She got quite hysterical before she finally departed.' He looked at her sideways, and still she wasn't sure if he were serious or not. 'I hope *you're* not an hysterical female, Gemma? One thing I can't tolerate is an excess of emotion.'

'Don't worry, Mr Durrant,' Gemma assured him, lifting her small chin in disdain. 'As far as I can see there's only one emotion I shall be likely to feel while I'm working for you.'

'Perhaps you'd better warn me? Or can I guess?' He really was smiling now—no question about it. He was, Gemma was forced to admit, extremely good-looking. A charmer too, with those dark-lashed eyes of his. She could imagine the kind of glamorous, sophisticated women who hung round him. No doubt they would put in an appearance soon—she was curious to see the kind of girl he would fall for.

'I would prefer not to continue this conversation,' she said primly. Then she saw the typewriter manual at the bottom of a drawer and pounced on it. 'Ah, this is what I needed. The cassettes? Yes, they're here. And the dictation machine is the same make as the one I've been using.'

He was still leaning back, his eyes fixed

unnervingly on her. 'In your last job?' he queried softly.

Gemma gulped. 'Yes, in my last job,' she said almost defiantly, sitting down and opening the manual, as a pointed hint that she would like to get on with her work.

But he didn't move. 'How old are you, Gemma?' he asked suddenly.

She looked up, startled. 'I—I'm twenty,' she lied. What was sixteen months more or less?

'I see. You're twenty. You have just left one job and were looking for another. You had several to choose from, of course, and were on the point of making up your mind when you happened to come in here yesterday about another matter.'

He was looking keenly at her now, and she didn't like his look, or his tone. She said nothing.

'That the picture, is it, Gemma?'

'Yes.' She stared at him, feeling her fingernails digging into her palms.

'Now,' he said softly, 'suppose you tell me the truth.'

'I don't know what you mean,' she whispered.

'I think you do. You're not a very convincing liar, Gemma.'

Oh well—this was the end, then. Poor old Beth's redundancy money would have to go to pay the wretched rates demand after all. Gemma stood up and re-covered the typewriter.

'All right,' she said. 'I'm eighteen. And eight months, if I must be exact. I haven't had another job; as a matter of fact I haven't quite finished my course at the secretarial school. I'm due to take my final exams in a month.' She picked up her handbag and turned to the door. 'I'm sorry I misled you and wasted your time, Mr Durrant. I'll see Mrs Brown on my way out and tell her——'

She was halfway to the door when he rapped out, 'Hold it!'

Gemma stopped and stood still, facing the door. His voice had a curious effect on her, it seemed to turn her to stone, like the characters in the old myths.

'Where do you think you're off to *now*?' he enquired wearily. 'There's one thing you must learn, my girl, if you're going to work for me, and that's restfulness. You really must get out of this habit of jumping about and making for the door on the least provocation.'

She turned very slowly. 'You mean—you still want to have me as your secretary?'

He sat down and leaned back in his chair. 'I probably want my head examined, but yes, I'm willing to take a chance. Now come back and sit down and tell me why you concocted that fancy story.'

She sat on the edge of the chair opposite. 'Well, I——' she bit the end of a scrupulously-manicured finger, a habit she had when deep in thought. 'I suppose it was really because of the rates demand. You see, Beth's salary is all we have to live on and keep the house going, and I was a bit angry about her having to use her—her hand-out, as you called it—to pay all the bills. She's been so wonderful to me all these years that I thought if I could get a job earlier than I expected to, then she could keep the money and use it for somethng she really wanted to do—like a trip abroad, or—or taking an art course, or something. You see, Beth's never really had any fun. So—so——' she bit the tip of her finger again '—when you took me by surprise by offering me the job, I thought——' her voice trailed off weakly as she met the grey eyes regarding her with an expression she couldn't interpret.

'Yes, I get the picture,' he said, and added brusquely, 'And don't do *that*.' He stretched across the desk and grasped her arm, jerking her finger from between her lips. 'Don't you know that's a provocative gesture? Or are you completely inexperienced in other ways—as well as in office work?' he added with heavy irony.

'Oh!' Gemma's deep blue eyes filled with tears, but she blinked them away quickly. He knew how to hurt, this man, how to make one look a fool. But the fact remained that the job was still on offer and she had to put up with him. 'I didn't know,' she said with a dignity that she wasn't aware of. 'I'll remember that in future.'

'Good,' he said shortly. 'Well, suppose we go on from where we left off, having wasted quite a quarter of an hour of office time, which I can't afford to do. The electronic typewriter—have a good look at it, study the manual, and see what you can make of it. The word-processor links on to the typewriter and you can use the whole works, or merely use the typewriter alone, at the flick of a switch. But the girl who comes to train you will explain all that to you. Meanwhile, have a go at the typewriter. If you really can't cope at all, tell me when I come in and I'll help you out. That quite clear?'

'Yes, Mr Durrant,' Gemma said meekly. She stood up and went back to the typing desk.

'Good,' he said again. 'I'll be down in the shop

if I'm wanted.' He strode over to the door. There he paused and turned back, with that odd smile curving his lashes. 'Chin up, Gemma,' he said. 'I'm not going to eat you, you know. But you needn't tell me any more lies, because I shall know if you do.' He went out and closed the door and she heard his footsteps running lightly down the wooden steps.

Gemma opened the thick manual of instructions. Her mind was spinning and at first she couldn't take anything in. What she needed was a strong cup of coffee to pull her wits together. It was a tremendous relief, though, that Harn Durrant knew the truth about her lack of experience. She had to admit that he had been quite decent about it. If only, she thought, she could somehow manage to cope with the work. She would like to—to *show* him. Oh lor', she groaned inwardly, here we go again! She really must get out of this childish habit of trying to prove something—she wasn't quite sure what.

Resolutely she turned her attention to the manual.

It really wasn't too difficult, she admitted half an hour later; not all that different from the modern electric machine she had been using at the college. Once she had mastered the way to set the margins and the line spacing she was ready to experiment with transcribing the letters. She plugged in the dictating machine, put in the first of the two cassettes from the top drawer, fixed the earphones and switched on.

To hear Harn Durrant's voice, firm and deep and so close that it had a curiously intimate quality, made her jump. It was as if he had leaned over her shoulder and put his head against hers. Don't be ridiculous, Gemma, she scolded herself, you're getting a fixation about the man. As he said, he's not going to eat you, so just get on with it.

The letters were straightforward, with hardly any deletions or corrections; he was obviously a man who didn't dither, but knew what he wanted to say and believed in getting it right the first time. Yes, that figured, that was what she would have expected. The text was all about paper, of course; about orders, delivery dates, shipments, invoices. Not too many technical terms, and what there were were familiar to Gemma. Beth had often brought work home in the years she had been employed here, and Gemma had sometimes typed letters for her on the small portable machine they kept at home. Beth had always checked them carefully, of course, and it had been practice for Gemma. Now it stood her in good stead, and terms like Aquarelle Canson and Rives Offset and Mould Made Bockingford were old friends. Using the typewriter wasn't quite so straightforward and she had to keep consulting the manual. It needed an even lighter touch than the electric machine she was used to, and it was so quiet that it seemed to be hardly working at all. At first the strip display alarmed her, but she very soon got used to that, and it was wonderful to be able to see the words appearing, glowing green on the narrow strip above the keyboard, before they were printed, so that any mistakes could be corrected before they were typed out.

In less than half an hour she had produced her first letter, and twenty minutes later two more were finished. She changed the cassette and started on the next batch, and her spirits rose with each letter accomplished. She could really cope—it was terrific! Harn Durrant's dictation was so clear and easily followed. He had an attractive voice, Gemma allowed herself to admit—deep and resonant. It could sound very sexy, she was sure— she giggled to herself as she wondered how he would speak to one of his numerous girl-friends. (Beth had told her they turned up all the time.)

She put a fresh wad of paper into the machine and flicked on the dictation again.

Then she went rigid. 'Darling girl,' she heard his voice, and she didn't need to wonder any longer how it would sound to someone he was in love with. It sounded tender and caressing and a couple of semitones deeper than before. This wasn't a business letter, of course, she didn't know what it was. 'Did you think of me today, and do you keep remembering last night—as I do all the time? Write me an answer to this—to see your writing is a thrill and a real letter is so much more satisfying than just a voice on the telephone. Love me? I adore you. Yours for ever and ever——'

That was the end of his dictation, the tape went silent. Gemma's toe slid weakly off the foot-control and an odd shock tingled through her. To hear his voice saying those words in that sexy tone, so close to her ear—it was quite shattering. Of course they weren't meant for her and she supposed she should be feeling guilty for listening. But she wasn't to know that this personal letter was on the tape he had given her to transcribe. She supposed he had written it out himself and forgotten to wipe it off the tape. She switched off the dictation machine and pulled off the headset.

Almost immediately she heard his step on the stairs outside and her heart missed a beat. He came straight across to her desk and picked up the pile of letters, glancing through them as he leafed them over. 'Very good,' he said. 'No problems with the machine?'

'I'm getting used to it,' she said. 'I shall get quicker with practice.'

'Good,' he said again. 'This the lot? I'll get them signed.' He turned back to his own desk.

'I——' Gemma began. 'There's just——'

'Yes?' he said sharply.

'There was another letter at the end of the second tape,' she said. Miserably she could feel her face going hot. 'It seemed to be a—a personal letter—I didn't know——'

'Oh, *that*! I thought I'd wiped it.' He glanced at her crimson cheeks. 'Poor Gemma, did it embarrass you? Don't give it another thought.'

He was actually laughing at her, the brute! In her most dignified 'secretary' voice she said, 'I take it you don't wish me to transcribe it?'

He was still chuckling. 'I haven't reached the stage yet of having my love-letters typewritten.' He was studying her face closely. 'You really *are* embarrassed, aren't you? Don't tell me you've never had a love-letter yourself.'

'I didn't think people still wrote love-letters,' she said, regaining her composure. 'Not when it's so easy to phone.'

'Ah, that's just the point. A girl can't kiss a phone call and put it under her pillow at night, can she? Whereas a letter has a certain permanence.

Come in!' as a tap sounded on the door.

Doris, apple-cheeked and frizzy-haired, the office girl who helped Mrs Brown, appeared with two cups on a tray. 'Your coffee, Mr Durrant, and Mrs Brown says to ask Miss Lawson if she takes sugar.'

Gemma smiled and shook her head and Harn Durrant said, deadpan, 'Miss Lawson is sweet enough without, don't you agree, Doris?'

The girl's eyes opened wide under their light-coloured lashes as she looked from him to Gemma and back again. Then, 'Ooh, Mr Durrant, you are a one!' she blurted out, and scuttled away down the stairs.

Harn Durrant perched on the edge of his desk and sipped his coffee, swinging one long leg pensively. 'I'd better put you in the picture, Gemma. I'll be away in London next week and I'll have to leave you to cope with any emergencies that may arise, deal with phone calls, make appointments. You've had your secretarial training—now this is the real thing, so just do your best. I'm not expecting anything vital to turn up. You'll be busy learning about the word-processor anyway. And if you really get stuck you'll have to consult Mrs Brown. That good lady is a tower of strength and common sense, but she has her hands full already, so don't waste her time unnecessarily.'

The intercom buzzed on his desk and Mrs Brown's voice said, 'Mr Underhill is here to see you, Mr Durrant.'

'Thanks, Mrs Brown. Send him up, please.' He turned to Gemma. 'Underhill's the architect who's hoping to get the contract for the alteration work I'm going to have done here—a reorganisation of the whole building. You'd better sit in on this interview and then you'll get an idea of how this place is going to look when it's finished. You can make notes for your own information if you like. The more you know about the business the better.'

There was a rather timid tap at the door and it opened to admit a tall, thin young man in cords and a polo sweater. He had an earnest expression and a flop of straight brown hair over a wide, clever brow. 'Morning, Mr Durrant.' He sat down on the edge of the chair that Harn Durrant waved him to, and put a bulging briefcase on the desk. 'Not too early, am I?' His eyes moved briefly towards Gemma, at the other end of the office, and away again.

Harn Durrant shook his head. 'All ready for you.' He sat down opposite. 'Oh, by the way, Derek, this is Gemma, my new secretary. She'll be in the office next week while I'm away, so you can leave any messages with her.'

The young architect half-rose from his chair, nodding and smiling. 'A pleasure, I'm sure.' His shy look of admiration was a boost to Gemma's confidence and she smiled back.

Harn Durrant's keen eyes had lost nothing of the small exchange of glances. 'Not *too* much of a pleasure, Derek. Gemma isn't just a pretty face, she'll have some demanding work to get through.'

The young man took that as a joke, although Gemma was fairly sure that it hadn't been meant as such. 'Ha, ha—yes, of course—no, I'm sure I shan't need to bother your secretary,' Derek Underhill laughed rather nervously.

'Mind you don't, then,' Harn Durrant said dryly. 'Now, have you got the revised plans for the administration department? Let's have a look at them.' The young man spread a plan out on the desk and Harn said over his shoulder, 'Gemma, you'd better come and sit beside me, and learn as much as you can about this.' He leaned over and drew up a chair close to his own, so close they were almost touching. Gemma came across the office and eased the chair a little further away from his, but before she could sit down he put out a hand and pulled it back to where it was before, without a word or a look in her direction.

Damn him, she thought, he's a mind-reader. He knows I don't want to sit that near to him. Reluctantly she sat down and was rewarded by a flicker of his lashes in her direction that might have been a kind of warning. Do as I say or else, he seemed to hint.

The meeting proceeded. Harn shot questions at the young architect, one after the other, hardly giving him time to reply, his arm reaching out across the plans on the desk, pointing to this item and that, criticising, objecting. Gemma felt sorry for the young man; she could see that he was getting more and more nervous under this onslaught. She was getting more and more nervous herself as the sleeve of Harn's jacket brushed her arm every time he stretched across the desk. She shrank back as far as she could in her chair, and he slanted her a glance from under those dark lashes that she could only call devilish. He was doing this on purpose, she realised. But why?

At last he sat back in his chair and gave Derek Underhill a withering look. 'This isn't really what I want at all—I explained it all at our last meeting. Can't you do any better than this?'

The young man flushed and muttered something about fire restrictions and the difficulty of obtaining certain materials that Mr Durrant had specified.

'Difficulties are there to be overcome,' Harn told him cuttingly.

Derek began to roll up the plans and Gemma saw that his hands weren't quite steady. In the end he dropped the plans on the floor. Bending to pick them up, he laughed rather selfconsciously. 'A bit clumsy this morning, I'm afraid, Mr Durrant,' he apologised. 'I was working on these most of last night.' He was laughing ruefully, it wasn't intended as an excuse.

Harn Durrant didn't laugh, he didn't even smile. He walked to the door and opened it. 'Then I suggest you might try a few more sleepless nights, in order to get somewhere near my requirements. If you want the job, that is,' he added, shrugging.

'Oh yes, I want the job, Mr Durrant,' Derek Underhill said quietly. His thin face had gone very pale now and Gemma thought he looked as if he might burst into tears.

'O.K., work on it while I'm away,' Harn Durrant said carelessly. 'Ring my secretary for an appointment.' He closed the door on the luckless young architect, whose steps could be heard stumbling down the wooden stairs.

Harn turned to Gemma, smiling. 'Well, did you pick up anything from all that? I don't imagine you did—the plans were miles away from what I specified. If young Underhill really stayed up all night working on them, I should think he'd dined too well first.'

'Were the plans really all that hopeless?' Gemma asked.

He shrugged. 'Not completely, but he has to be kept up to the mark or he'll get carried away by his own inventiveness. He has some very good ideas and I like that, but I also intend to keep him on a very tight rein. He's only beginning, you see, he has his way to make and he badly needs this commission.'

Gemma stood up. 'Poor young man,' she sighed. 'He was rather upset. You really hurt his feelings, didn't you?'

Harn Durrant walked slowly back to the desk, staring at her incredulously. 'His *feelings*? What have feelings to do with it? Feelings are a self-indulgence that have no place where matters of business are concerned.' He snapped the rubber band over his notebook and thrust it into his pocket. Then he looked suspiciously at Gemma as she stood observing him as if he were a strange animal in a zoo. The ability to feel was something that distinguished a human being from a wild animal, surely? Where did that leave Harn Durrant?

'What's the matter?' he asked impatiently.

'Oh, nothing, nothing at all.' Gemma walked back to her own desk and sat down.

He came after her and stood behind her chair. 'You're very young, Gemma, and working for me will be a baptism of fire, I promise you. But if you can manage to see things my way, and not through a rosy haze of sentimentality, like most girls of your age, I think we may get along very well.' He put hands on her shoulders and gave them a quick squeeze. 'O.K.?'

The touch of his hard fingers through her thin blouse gave her a curious sensation that was mostly pleasurable. Was that being sentimental? No, she thought, she had no feeling for this man at all, except perhaps contempt, if that could be reckoned a feeling.

'O.K.,' she said coolly. A thought was beginning to take shape in her mind, and it was an uncomfortable thought. Why had he drawn up her chair so close to his, so that when he stretched forward he would be bound to touch her arm or her hand? Why did he find it necessary to put his hands on her shoulders when he was encouraging her? Why (and this was the most unpleasant possibility of all) had he got rid of Beth, who was thirty-four, and engaged instead a young girl who might be much more compliant—much more likely to be bowled over by his undoubted charisma? Gemma felt herself go hot and cold as an obvious answer to this last question suggested itself. Already he had accused her of being provocative. What sort of a girl did he think she was? Accommodating?

I'm certainly not going to be *that* kind of secretary, she assured herself, moving forward so that his hands slipped from her shoulders. If that's what he's looking for he'll have to look elsewhere. Her pretty lips set into a firm line as she said, 'Have you any more work for me, Mr Durrant, or shall I go on practising on the typewriter?'

He perched himself on the end of her desk, next to the word-processor, and placed his hand on the top of the screen almost affectionately.

'I think perhaps I'd better take a little time off to put you in the picture,' he said. 'But not at this moment. I've got several long-distance phone calls booked that will probably take me up to lunchtime. I suggest that you come out and have a snack lunch with me and I'll give you all the gen. You've got to be familiar with my proposed plans for the future of the business if you're to be any use to me.'

The phone rang on his desk and he went over to it. 'Yes, Mrs Brown? From New York? Right, put him though, please.'

He placed a hand over the mouthpiece and spoke to Gemma. 'You go along down to Ted and learn all you can from him about his side of things. I'll collect you when I'm ready.' Without a pause he spoke into the telephone. 'Josh? Hullo, how are you? Fine, thanks. Now, about that contract——'

Gemma got up and went quietly out of the office.

Ted was delighted to see her. Business was slack at the moment, he told her, but he guessed that young Mr Durrant was going to liven things up pretty soon. 'He's got a finger in several pies, that one. He's off to London next week.'

'Yes, he told me,' said Gemma, and went on to explain that she was the new temporary secretary. 'Mr Durrant sent me down to learn a bit about what goes on in your department.' She quirked a smile at the elderly man. 'After all, this is the most important part of the business, isn't it? Where the action is, as they say.'

Ted chuckled delightedly and smoothed back his thinning hair. 'I can see you've got the right idea, Miss Gemma. Well now, you come along with me and I'll show you the stock books and the store room. I pride myself,' he added modestly, 'that I can find my way round here in the dark—I can put my hand on any piece of paper, any ream, any bale, at a moment's notice.'

'I bet you can, Ted,' Gemma smiled.

Half an hour later she enlarged on that. 'You're a marvel,' she said as they made their way back to the shop. 'You've got it all taped, haven't you?'

'It's been my life for forty-two years, Miss Gemma,' Ted told her. 'You sort of grow fond of the different sorts of paper, if that doesn't sound silly. Sometimes I try to picture the great forests—in Canada maybe, where the paper started as trees. And then I begin to think as it was a pity to have to cut those trees down. But I guess that's just being soft.' He grinned ruefully. 'You can't afford to be soft in business, can you, Miss Gemma?'

'No, I suppose you can't,' she sighed. That was the second time this morning she had heard that view expressed, but in very different circumstances. Ted had a heart, no doubt about that. The man upstairs had only his cool, calculating intelligence. No heart—not for business at any rate. But out of business hours? The words of that letter came back to her and she heard again his voice, low and sexy, saying, 'I adore you.'

'Ready, Gemma?' She hadn't heard him come downstairs, and the clipped tones, so different from the voice in her head, made her jump.

'Er—yes, quite ready, Mr Durrant.' She turned to Ted and thanked him for showing her round the stores.

'My pleasure, Miss Gemma.' Ted went back to his stock-book.

'A good fellow, Ted Baines,' Harn remarked briskly as he led the way to his Mercedes. 'There isn't much he doesn't know about the business.'

'He's a poppet,' Gemma said warmly as he slid into the driving seat beside her.

He pursed his lips. 'Um—yes. Possibly,' he said, and as the car nosed its way out into the High Street he added, 'You have a very subjective view of people, don't you, Gemma?'

She kept her eyes straight ahead as they threaded their way through the traffic. 'If you mean do I consider people as human beings, with feelings, yes, I suppose I do.'

'Still on about the way I treated your stepsister?' he enquired mildly.

'You asked me a question and I answered it,' she said in a crisp voice.

He laughed out loud. 'I can see I'm going to have to watch my step with you, Gemma! You're not afraid of me, are you? I like that.'

She glanced up at the straight back, at the squared shoulders and the hard line of his mouth, and she thought, I could be afraid of you. She hoped nothing would happen to bring that about.

'We'll go to the lunch-buffet place at the Dennington,' he said, turning into the car-park of the town's most prestigious hotel. 'They put on quite a good choice and you don't have to wait about to be served. You know it?'

'Good heavens, no,' said Gemma as they walked in through the heavy swing doors. 'This isn't my scene at all. Much too pricey.'

A waft of expensive perfume came to meet them, followed by a girl who came running along the softly-carpeted corridor. She wore a floaty lavender outfit and her ash-blonde hair waved and curled round baby-soft cheeks. Her lips parted in a brilliant smile as she reached Harn and put a hand on his shoulder, lifting her pretty face in a gesture that asked for a kiss. She didn't seem to notice Gemma.

'Harn—darling! I guessed right. I thought you might be coming in for lunch. I've got a table—*our* table by the window.' She spoke quickly, nervously, the words tumbling over each other with a false gaiety.

Gemma drew away and stood beside a door that led into a bar. The girl didn't seem to realise that Harn wasn't alone. Gemma supposed this must often happen to a secretary, and the thing to do was to fade into the background. She was standing half turned away from the pair, but she didn't think that Harn accepted the invitation to kiss the girl and it was impossible to miss the coldness in his voice as he said, 'Sorry, Julia. We're not lunching together today or any day in the future. I thought I made that clear last night.'

'But you didn't mean it—you couldn't—not after—there was some sort of misunderstanding, wasn't there?' The voice shook with pleading. 'You were worried about business, that was it, wasn't it? Harn darling, tell me you didn't mean it! I couldn't bear——' The voice cracked and broke on a sob.

'Oh, for Pete's sake, Julia, don't make a scene. It's over, that's all there is to say. You knew the score all along, so don't start whining about it now.'

The callousness in his voice made Gemma wince. She looked briefly at the girl standing holding on to the door-frame as if she needed support. Her face was ghastly and there were dark smudges under her eyes, which were swimming in tears.

'I suggest you go home,' Harn said stonily. 'Are you alone? Come along then, I'll see you out to your car.' He looked round. 'Gemma, where are you? Oh, there you are.' Quite deliberately, it seemed, he rested his hand for a moment on her waist. 'Wait here for me, there's a dear girl.'

He took Julia's arm in a tight grasp and pushed her towards the door. As she turned, Julia seemed to see Gemma for the first time. She stared for a moment, her tear-drenched violet eyes flying wide with a kind of horror. Then she made an odd, whimpering noise and stumbled through the doorway into the car-park, Harn still holding her arm in a pitiless grasp.

He was back in a couple of minutes. 'Sorry about that,' he said briefly, and led the way into the bar. 'Let's have a drink before we eat.'

The bar was crowded and Gemma stood wedged in a corner while Harn fought his way to the bar. He nodded to the one or two men who greeted him on the way, but didn't speak or stop.

'Here you are—lemonade.' He thrust a tall glass into her hand. 'That do you?' He added carelessly, 'You're too young for alcohol at lunchtime.'

She would have asked for lemonade anyway, but he might have consulted her and not treated her like a little girl. But he looked so moody and unapproachable as he tossed off his whisky that she thanked him meekly and made no comment.

The luncheon room had a long buffet table down the side, presided over by a chef in a tall white hat. The savoury dishes looked so luscious and tempting that Gemma forgot the nasty little scene that had just taken place in the realisation that she was very hungry indeed.

'What will you have?' asked Harn. 'You might like the ham and mushroom quiche. Yes?' He indicated a creamy-looking dish and she agreed eagerly. 'Roll and butter? Salad? O.K. You go and grab that table over by the window and I'll bring it across.'

She did as he told her. As she sat down she thought, with a quirk of humour, that she was behaving like his poodle, following behind obediently. But of course that was what he was paying her for—this wasn't a social lunch date. She must never let herself think of him as a human being, with feelings, because he had shown pretty plainly that he hadn't got any.

As he came down the long room towards her, carrying a tray, she thought absently that he made all the other men in the room look ordinary. As he put the tray down on the table he smiled at her and she thought how white his teeth were in the lean, sun-tanned cheeks. Then, immediately, followed the thought, This is how it must have been in the beginning with the girl Julia. They would sit here, probably at this same table, and she would look up as see him coming towards her and her heart would throb.

Poor Julia, thought Gemma, remembering the way Harn had shrivelled the girl up with a look. If he ever looked at me like that I should want to die.

But that wouldn't happen, of course. Their relationship, such as it was, was entirely different. He was the big boss and she was his secretary—on probation for a month. He was a man of the world and he would never see her—Gemma—as anything more than a young girl hardly out of school, and quite unused to the ways of his sophisticated world and its inhabitants. And of course she would never, for a moment, want him to.

Would she?

As an alarming thought occurred to her she began to lift the tip of one slender finger to her lips. Then she remembered and quickly put it down again. The last thing she wanted was to be accused of being provocative. That would get her nowhere with Harn Durrant. Or rather, it would probably get her out of her job in double quick time.

There was only one safe way to relate to the heartless brute, and that was to meet him on his own ground. It wasn't going to be easy to pretend to be cool, aloof, detached, but if that would help her to keep the job she could at least try.

And as she cut into the deliciously creamy quiche that he set before her, Gemma found, rather to her surprise, that she would be desperately disappointed, now, if he were to dismiss her.

CHAPTER THREE

HARN ate his veal pie in brooding silence for a time. Then he put down his knife and fork and said, 'I can't let that little episode with Julia pass without a word or two, Gemma. I can foresee that she might possibly turn up at the office, and you'd better be prepared to deal with her.'

Cool, aloof, detached, Gemma reminded herself, that was what she had to be. She lifted her prettily-marked eyebrows and said, 'Is it part of my job, then, to deal with discarded girl-friends?'

He let out a short, bitter laugh. 'Oh yes, indeed. Didn't they warn you at your college that a secretary must be prepared to protect her chief from unwelcome callers?'

She broke off a piece of roll and buttered it carefully. 'Yes, I do see what you mean. Will there be many of them?' she enquired innocently. 'Discarded girl-friends, I mean. If so, I must think out a technique for getting rid of them.'

Harn scowled. 'Are you being funny at my expense, young lady? Because if so——'

'No, of course not,' she said hastily. 'I'm merely asking for information.' She met his frown with limpid blue eyes. 'I would naturally expect a man like you to have a good many girl-friends, discarded or not.'

'What exactly do you mean—a man like me?'

She examined his lean, handsome face thoughtfully. 'Well, you're—you know—macho, sexy.'

'Really?' He leaned towards her, eyebrows raised. 'And how would you know that at your tender age, Gemma?'

She popped the piece of roll into her mouth, crunched it, and shrugged. 'Feminine intuition, they call it.'

'I see.' He was suddenly curt. 'Well, don't let your feminine intuition run away with you, that's all. And as far as Julia Moore goes, you needn't imagine that she's been treated badly. Poor Julia's somewhat thick, and there's only one way to deal with a girl like that—state everything in words of one syllable so that she gets the message.' His mouth hardened. 'When a girl throws herself at a man and clings on, she's only got herself to blame for the consequences. I've always made it quite clear that I'm definitely not in the marriage market, which was what Julia had in mind. Now, suppose we get down to business? That was what I brought you out to lunch for.'

'Of course.' Gemma looked demurely down at the table. 'Shall I take notes—I've got a notepad in my handbag.'

'No,' he barked. Then, with a glance at the crowded tables around, he repeated more quietly, 'No, there's no need. This is a general briefing.'

Gemma nodded meekly and was silent.

He finished his pie and pushed the plate aside. 'Firstly,' he said, 'you may be wondering about my previous connection with the business?'

Gemma nodded. 'Yes, I couldn't understand why Beth never mentioned you all these years, and why I never saw you when I came to the office.'

'That's easily explained—I hadn't been to the office for many years until my father died. We needn't go into the family history, but the fact is that my parents were divorced when I was very young. My mother remarried and I grew up with her and my stepfather. I went into my stepfather's business, which was electronics, and when he retired a few years ago I took over the management of his firm. We lived outside London and I used to come up to visit my father quite frequently, but I never took any part in his business here.' He smiled rather bleakly. 'He didn't think much of modern technology and I'm sure he believed that the electronics industry was the curse of our age. He liked everything old and traditional, which is why the office here is quite a time-capsule. He wouldn't have anything altered.'

Gemma said slowly, 'I see now why he got on so well with Beth. She loves old things too. Sometimes Ted used to give her a few sheets of beautiful thick handmade paper that had got damaged and was unfit for sale, and she would write on them in script and paint exquisite decorations—you know, like they used to do in the old monasteries. But—but surely you're not going to change everything, are you? I mean, Durrants has a splendid reputation for the very best paper? Beth has always said people come from all over the country to get some particular paper they want.'

He leaned back, watching her under lowered eyelids. 'I don't quite see myself as a monk.' His dark lashes flickered so that she couldn't tell if he were smiling or not. 'But I've decided to carry on with the paper business here—for a time at least—rather than sell it, and I can't possibly work in an office that comes straight out of a Charles Dickens novel. On the other hand, I agree that it would be unwise to make any major alterations to the shop, or to the worthy Mrs Brown's department downstairs. It would be quite possible to computerise there, but Mrs Brown would never accept it, and I quite understand that. But for my own office work I intend to have the kind of technology I'm used to. That's why your sister wouldn't do. She would never have adapted to what I have in mind—as I think you'll agree, if you're honest. It will be a long, long way from a monastery.'

He was definitely smiling now. Gemma's breath caught in her throat as she met the full impact of that smile. Heavens, but the man was dynamite! No wonder he had a trail of girls languishing for him, and she pitied them.

She felt her cheeks begin to flush and put her napkin to her mouth quickly. 'So that's why you took *me* on, was it? Because I *didn't* come straight out of a Dickens novel?' She scraped the last bits of the quiche together industriously.

'That was one of the reasons.' She could feel his eyes still fixed on her, although she was concentrating on her plate. There was quite a silence, then he added, in a brisker tone, 'You strike me as a girl who's quite at home in the modern age, and anyway I prefer to have a secretary that I can train in my own ways from scratch, rather than have to undo all the bad habits that an experienced girl would probably have picked up.'

Gemma lifted her eyes to meet his then. It took quite an effort. '*One* of the reasons? Am I to be allowed to know the others?'

His lips twisted sardonically. 'Bright child, aren't you?' He looked at her empty plate and asked, 'Would you like anything in the pudding line? Gateau? Ice cream?'

She was evidently not going to be told the other reasons, whatever they were. 'I'd love an ice cream.' She might as well enjoy all the perks of the job while she had the chance. She probably wouldn't have it long.

'And coffee?'

'Thank you. White.'

For the rest of the meal the talk was entirely of business. Gemma tried to concentrate as Harn explained the contracts that were in the offing; the ones that were tied up and due to be executed; and itemised what she might expect to receive in the way of correspondence. 'Yes,' she said. 'Yes, I understand,' and she nodded at intervals. But she found herself watching his face instead of listening carefully to what he was saying. The way his dark lashes curved upwards at the corners of his eyes fascinated her. She wondered idly what he would be like if this were a social occasion instead of a working lunch, if it were the beginning of one of his numerous affairs, and she heard his voice again whispering, 'Love me? I adore you.'

She pulled herself together with a jerk as she heard him saying, 'That puts you in the picture for next few days, while I'm away. I don't expect miracles, but do your best. And I'll be interested to hear how you get on with the word-processor. Now, have you finished? Come along, then, let's get back.'

Gemma picked up her handbag obediently and followed him out of the hotel.

Beth was hovering in the hall of their neat little semi on the outskirts on the small town when Gemma opened the front door at six o'clock that evening. She took Gemma's bag and jacket and led her into the living room, almost as if she were an invalid. 'Well,' she enquired anxiously, 'how did it go?' She was obviously expecting the worst.

Gemma slumped into an armchair. 'Not bad. Not at all bad, really.' She had been thinking hard all the way home, and she had worked out just how much she could tell Beth. 'I found the new typewriter a bit of a mystery at first, but in the end I managed to get the hang of it, more or less. There wasn't a great deal to do, fortunately, just a few letters, so I was able to spend the rest of the time studying the manual and practising. Mr Durrant is arranging for someone to come from London to train me on the word-processor.' She pulled a face. 'I expect the crunch will come then.'

Beth's soft brown eyes regarded her with relief and admiration. 'You're a wonder, Gem! I can't thank you enough for stepping into the breach. Come and eat, I've got tea all ready.' She led the way into the kitchen. 'I'm doing scrambled eggs, will that be enough for you? Did you go to the Magpie's Nest for lunch as usual?' The two girls usually patronized a café in the town that put on a good cooked lunch at a moderate price, which saved the trouble of cooking when they got home in the evening.

'Well—no. I mean, yes, scrambled eggs will do beautifully. But no, I didn't go to the Magpie's Nest.' Gemma laughed a little selfconsciously. 'As a matter of fact I was taken out to lunch by the boss. To the buffet at the Dennington, believe it or not!'

'*No!*' Beth turned from the cooker, wooden spoon raised, mouth falling open, and Gemma went on hastily.

'It's O.K., Sis, nothing sinister afoot! He only wanted to brief me on the running of the office, and he was too darned busy to take time off during office hours to do it. I had a gorgeous mushroom quiche,' she added, rolling her eyes.

'Well!' Beth exclaimed, and that seemed all she was capable of saying. She finished the scrambled eggs, spooned them on to toast and carried the plates to the table. Then she looked across at Gemma and smiled crookedly. 'Sorry, Gemma love, I didn't mean to play the heavy elder sister. It's just that I know that man Durrant. He's a womaniser, no doubt about that. In the short time I was working with him there've been at least three different girls ringing him up, calling at the office for him in the evening. You don't tell me he hasn't encouraged them,' she added, with a disapproving shrug.

Gemma thought of poor Julia. He certainly hadn't encouraged her—or maybe he had, at the beginning. She remembered that letter: 'Darling girl—love me? I adore you.' Was that for Julia, or had he got another girl-friend by the time he wrote that? Most probably he had, she decided, and was conscious of a small uneasy disturbance inside herself that she couldn't account for. It didn't concern her, of course, how many girl-friends the man had. Unless he expected her to be constantly involving herself in shaking them off when he got tired of them. He really was a callous brute, Gemma told herself—heartless, utterly self-centred, the type of man she had always disliked and avoided.

She smiled at Beth now. 'Don't let's talk about *him*,' she said. 'It's impossible to like the man, but I can put up with him for a while, if it suits me. Now, let's talk about you. What have you been doing with yourself today, and are you feeling better?'

'Thanks to you—much better. Although I've

been a bit worried about letting you take my job on. I feel guilty, I shouldn't have let you do it, I should have gone back today and worked out my month's notice. And His Nibs would have to have had to put up with his letters typed on the old Remington.'

Gemma chuckled as she applied herself energetically to the scrambled eggs. 'Don't worry about me, Sis, I'm sure I can cope. And it's probably good for me to be thrown in at the deep end. It's a challenge.'

Beth sighed and shook her head. 'Just don't let him push you around too much, that's all. He'll try it on, you know.'

'I won't,' Gemma told her firmly. But in her mind she saw vividly a picture of a pair of thickly-lashed grey eyes regarding her in a curiously intent way that made her feel weak inside, and she added to herself, 'I hope I won't.'

The next day was Friday. Gemma called in at the secretarial college early, on her way to the office, and explained the position. Her tutor was impressed and offered her congratulations that Gemma had got herself such a good job, even if only temporary.

'I'll keep you on the register for six months,' she said. 'Then, if you want to take the exams you could take them at Christmas, probably. Anyway, keep in touch and let me know how you get on and if you need any advice.'

Gemma made her way to the office of Durrants (Fine Paper) Ltd. feeling that there was any amount of advice she needed, but perhaps not quite the kind that Miss Benson had in mind.

Again, Harn was in the office before her, sitting at his desk. Gemma had spent a good deal of the time since yesterday thinking about him, and what it would be like to work for him, to be in contact with him day after day. And now she saw him again this morning the reality was stunning. He really was fabulously attractive, she had to admit, her quick glance taking in the dark, well-groomed hair, the lean cheeks, and those thick, sweeping lashes that for the moment hid his eyes as his head bent over his desk.

He looked up and she met the full impact of his eyes, the steely grey eyes with the darker rims round the iris, that she found so unnerving.

'Good morning, Mr Durrant.' She turned away quickly and hung up her light jacket on the old-fashioned coat-stand in the corner. 'Sorry I'm a little late. I had to let them know at the college that I shouldn't be coming in again for the present.'

He nodded briefly. 'O.K. Let's get on, then.'

He gave her a wad of scribbled notes to type. 'See what you do with those. No need to set them out elaborately. When you've got them typed let me know and I'll mark them for you to set out finally in the proper order. I need them to take with me to London.'

Gemma busied herself with the task and had it finished in under an hour. She drew the last page out of the machine with a sigh of relief and looked up to see Harn Durrant regarding her from the other end of the office.

'Finished?'

She nodded and got to her feet, but before she could take the notes to him he was walking across to her desk. The side window looked over the yard where the staff cars were parked and he glanced down through it as he passed. She heard his quick intake of breath, and the next moment he bent his head over the sheets of paper she had just typed.

'Good,' he said. 'You're a clever girl, Gemma.' His voice sounded odd.

Quick footsteps could be heard running up the wooden stairs outside the office. Harn moved closer to Gemma. 'And a pretty one too,' he added softly.

What happened next was so unexpected it took her breath away completely. She felt his arm slip round her waist and his mouth come down to cover hers in a kiss so hard that she was unable to move her head away. He drew her close and held her in a steely grip, pressed tightly against the long, hard length of him. Gemma struggled to move one leg, which was all that was free, for his arms were wrapped around her arms, pinning them to her sides. But it was a feeble gesture, and useless, for his own leg immediately wound itself round hers, anchoring it even more securely. She was suffocating, drowning, her head buzzing.

Then, from behind them, came the sound of the office door bursting open. After a long moment Harn took his mouth away from Gemma's, but still his arms held her close. Weakly she twisted her head round, to see a girl in a green dress standing in the doorway. Julia!

The girl stood there, staring at the scene before her, her face ashen, under the white-gold hair, patches of crimson on each cheek. Her eyes were fixed and wide, as if in shock, and her mouth moved convulsively.

It was like a silent tableau, the three of them standing motionless. The girl spoke first. 'So that's it!' she spat out. 'And you hadn't the guts to tell me you had another girl!' Her lips drew together, her eyes narrowed and her hand went to her throat as if it hurt her. 'You're a bastard, Harn Durrant—an utter bastard!'

She stood for another second or two, but when Harn still didn't move or speak she let out a small sound like a wounded animal and stumbled from the office and down the stairs.

Harn released Gemma immediately and went over and closed the door. Then he turned with a wry shrug and seemed about to say something, but Gemma spoke first. 'That's my opinion of you too,' she burst out, and put a hand to her burning cheeks. 'You did that deliberately, of course. You just *used* me. I think you're absolutely disgusting!'

He walked back to her slowly. 'Do you, Gemma?' he said quietly. 'Do you really? That's a pity, because I was thinking that *you* are quite delightful. I must admit, though, that it wasn't much of a kiss. I can do better than that. Let me show you.'

His arm went round her waist again, drawing her close, and he was smiling into her eyes in a way that had a stupefying effect on her. Her head reeled. Where had she read that the great jungle beasts hypnotised their prey before they struck the fatal blow? 'N-no,' she whispered as his head came nearer. She fixed her eyes on his mouth, on his lips. Never before had she felt this weakness, this hunger. If his mouth didn't touch hers she would die.

'Yes,' he whispered in that low sexy voice she

had heard on the tape. Nearer and nearer his lips approached hers. She closed her eyes and let out a little moan as she felt their touch, gentle, probing, his mouth brushing against hers slowly and deliberately. Gemma had been kissed before—of course she had—boys' kisses, clumsy, fumbling, shy—but this man was an expert. He knew the way to arouse a woman. He was taking a mean, despicable advantage of her. Even while somewhere at the back of her mind she acknowledged all this, still her body responded; her lips parted to his kiss, her arms went up round his neck, pressing his head down to hers. It was as natural as breathing. She hadn't known—oh, she hadn't known, she thought dizzily, that her body could strain and ache like this.

She wanted it to go on forever, and when he finally put her away from him very gently she felt cold and lost.

'There,' he said. 'How was that?'

She turned her head away, pressing her knuckles childishly against her mouth, fighting back tears.

'Gemma?' He came close again.

'Go away,' she blurted, but he took her shoulders and turned her round to face him.

'Gemma, you're crying! My infant, it was only a kiss. It meant nothing. Don't upset yourself, for goodness' sake.'

'I'm not upset,' she sniffed. 'I just think you're beastly, that's all. Like I said, you used me to show that Julia girl that you're through with her and I think it was a horrible, mean thing to do!'

Harn wrinkled his brow as if this was a new and strange thought to him. 'Was it? It seemed to me the obvious thing at that moment, if we didn't want to witness another melodramatic scene.' He chuckled. 'It worked, anyway, you can't deny that.'

Gemma blew her nose. 'Don't you ever think about anyone but yourself?' she said coldly.

He shrugged. 'That's a hard way of putting it, but—no, when I come to consider it, I don't suppose I do. But don't let's start arguing about that. Now, forget what's just happened, there's a good girl. I shouldn't think Julia will give us any more trouble.' He walked over to the desk and picked up the notes she had been typing. 'Now, to work, where were we? Oh yes, I was going to put these notes in order, wasn't I?'

Gemma drew a deep breath. Perhaps she was getting worked up about nothing. As he said, it was only a kiss—the way it had happened it was a sort of joke to him.

But at the back of her mind there was a nagging little thought beginning to take shape—that to her it hadn't been a joke at all. It had been the beginning of something new and rather frightening.

Harn was leaving at midday for London, and the remainder of the morning passed in a flurry of telephone calls and last-minute instructions. He was travelling by train, and Gemma had already ordered a taxi to take him to the station. When Mrs Brown rang up to say that it had arrived Gemma sighed with relief. Her initiation into what it meant to be a secretary to a jet-age, go-getting chief was proving somewhat exhausting.

'Your taxi's here, Mr Durrant,' she called through to his cloakroom along the passage.

He came out carrying his hand-baggage, his eyes

shining like polished flint. He was off on a trip and he was going to enjoy every minute of it. He might have been going to meet a lover, Gemma thought. Perhaps he was, followed the second thought, and she felt again that twinge she had felt before; not jealousy, of course, that would have been quite absurd. She couldn't put a name to it.

'O.K. then, I'm off. You've got all the gen? Right. Do your best, Gemma. Be good.' Surprisingly, he bent and kissed the top of her head before he turned and clattered down the wooden stairs. She heard his voice in the shop, then the slam of the taxi door, and when she turned and walked slowly back into the office it seemed curiously empty.

She stood in the middle of the long room thoughtfully biting on the tip of one finger. It couldn't be possible that she was going to miss him, could it? She pushed the thought aside. Of course she wasn't, she was *glad* he wouldn't be here. Perhaps what she would miss was something dynamic about him, an aliveness that seemed to link with something in herself that she hadn't—until now—suspected.

'Oh, I don't know,' she said aloud, impatiently. She would concentrate on her work and forget about the man himself, as he had no doubt already forgotten about her.

As she began to tidy up his desk there was a tap on the door and it opened a little way to disclose the diffident face of the young architect, Derek Underhill, under the flop of brown hair. He looked to right and to left, then 'Hullo,' he mouthed silently, seeing Gemma. And—jerking his thumb towards Harn's desk—'Has he gone?'

She grinned. 'Yes, he's gone. Come in.'

The young man advanced into the office, pantomiming relief. 'Good. I didn't want to run into any more snags and objections from your chief today. I came back because I'm missing a list of specifications that was clipped onto one of the plans I had spread out on the desk, earlier on. Have you come across it, by any chance?'

Gemma picked up a slip of paper from Harn's desk. 'Is this it? I've just noticed it.'

'Eureka! Yes, that's the little beauty. How clever of you to find it. You must be the perfect secretary.' He gave her a frankly admiring glance. 'Isn't she supposed to be able to lay her hand on anything at a moment's notice?'

Gemma laughed. 'I doubt if I'd qualify, not yet anyway. I've only been a secretary for two half-days.'

He leaned against the desk, regarding her with disbelief. 'Really? You're not pulling my leg? You seem very cool and competent to me.'

'That's just a bold front.' Gemma smiled wryly. 'Actually, I'm dithering inside most of the time.' She walked down the office and began to put together the papers on her own desk.

Derek Underhill followed and stood watching her. After a moment's silence he said, 'I imagine friend Durrant isn't the easiest of men to work for. I expect you need a bold front.'

That was a blatant quiz. He couldn't have failed to notice the way Harn had pulled up her chair close to his, the way he had deliberately touched her arm as he stretched across the desk.

She said nothing, and after another silence, longer this time, Derek picked up a Biro from the desk and twiddled it between finger and thumb. 'Would you give me you advice on something if I asked you?'

Gemma turned surprised blue eyes on him. 'Me—advise you? It sounds very unlikely but—'doubtfully'—I suppose I would if I could. About what?'

He said quickly, 'Look, you haven't had lunch yet, have you? Would you share a sandwich with me and I'd explain?'

'Well——' Gemma hesitated. Derek Underhill seemed a pleasant, inoffensive young man, but if he was going to try to involve her in any way about the plans for the new office it might be awkward. Her loyalty was to Harn Durrant, her employer, bully though he might be.

'*Please*,' pleaded the young man, and Gemma hadn't the heart to put him down.

'All right,' she said. 'But I doubt if I can help you. If it's anything to do with the plans for the new building, I can't——'

'No, not really,' he said quickly. 'This isn't industrial espionage or anything dramatic like that, I promise you.'

Gemma laughed and picked up her handbag. 'Right then, let's go!'

On the way out she put her head inside Mrs Brown's office. 'Just going out for a bite of lunch, Mrs Brown. I'll only be half an hour or so and I've locked the office upstairs. That all right with you?' She put the key on Mrs Brown's desk.

That lady raised her head from a hefty accounts book she was writing in, in a beautifully neat hand, and said, 'I usually go at one. Be back by then, will you, dear?' She smiled and added, 'He got off all right, then?'

Gemma pulled a face. 'Rather a rush at the end, but we got through.'

Mrs Brown raised her eyebrows meaningly. 'We'll have a bit of peace for a few days, then.' She went back to her accounts book.

Gemma joined Derek Underhill outside and they walked to a sandwich bar in the High Street and settled down at a corner table with coffees and a plate of sandwiches between them.

Derek smiled across the table at Gemma. 'This is nice and friendly. I'm glad Durrant didn't want to take you to London with him.'

Gemma gave him a direct look. 'Why should he?'

'Oh well——' he flushed faintly '—men do take their pretty secretaries around with them, I've noticed.' He pulled a contrite face as he saw her expression. 'Sorry if I've spoken out of turn.'

'You have,' Gemma said shortly. She felt angry, but not with Derek. With Harn Durrant for having deliberately given the wrong impression, not once but twice. 'What did you want to ask me about, Mr Underhill?'

'Oh, *Derek*, please,' he said. 'Look, don't hold it against me, Gemma, and I may call you Gemma, mayn't I? It was just my way of making sure I wasn't treading on any toes.'

He really did look sorry, and Gemma relented. 'No toes,' she smiled. 'But what about the advice?'

He glanced uncertainly at her and away again. 'I'm afraid I've not made a very good start. The fact is that you'll think this is awful cheek, I expect, but—well, actually it *is* connected with my meeting with your boss this morning.' He put a finger into the collar of his white polo sweater and eased it away from his throat. 'I wondered if you might be able to tell me if it was finally thumbs-down after I left the office this morning, that's all.'

The café was filling up now, noisy with chatter and the clink of crockery. Outside the wide plate-glass window a queue of cars panted at the traffic-lights. Gemma frowned down at her plate and wondered what she could say. Confidentiality was, she had been taught, something that is first and foremost expected of a secretary.

'I'm sorry,' she said at last, 'I'm afraid I can't help you. I don't know what's in Mr Durrant's mind, and if I did I don't think it would be right for me to discuss it.'

He pulled a very wry face. 'That puts me in my place, doesn't it? But I suppose you're right. It's just that—well, I've staked rather a lot on getting this work, and if Mr Durrant intends to turn me down flat I'd rather know straight away. But never mind that, I know I shouldn't have asked.'

Disappointment was written all over his face, but he was trying his best to conceal it. And suddenly Gemma changed her mind. She believed that people did their best if you encouraged them, not bawled them out.

Impulsively she said, 'I don't know anything for sure, of course, but I don't think he's made up his mind yet.' She thought for a moment and then added rather recklessly, 'As a matter of fact, he told me after you'd gone that he thought some of your ideas were pretty good.'

If she had felt any guilt it disappeared as she saw the young man's face light up. 'Oh, bless you, Gemma, you're a sport! I'll work like mad on those plans, and I can have two or three alternative ideas ready by the time Mr Durrant gets back from London.' He leaned towards her and added confidentially, 'It's not easy to get started in this profession, you know. I've had one or two small commissions, but this one would give me a real boost. Durrants' name carries a good bit of weight around this town.'

When they parted at the shop door a little later he squeezed her hand. 'Thanks again, Gemma, you'll never know how you've bucked me up. Perhaps,' he added tentatively, 'I could stand you lunch again and tell you how I'm getting on?'

It wasn't the first time Gemma had seen that look in a young man's eyes. She liked Derek, but she didn't want to start anything with him; she had enough on her plate just now. 'I'm going to be very busy while Mr Durrant's away,' she said. 'I can't promise anything.' She smiled at him to soften her refusal.

He held her hand a little longer before he let it go. 'Oh well, I'll be seeing you,' he said, and stood watching her grey skirt swinging round her long slender legs as she walked into the shop.

At five o'clock that afternoon Gemma saw the white sports car parked on the opposite side of the road as soon as she came out of the shop doorway. She glanced at it only briefly. She didn't include in her circle of acquaintances anyone who owned a car as expensive as that. She felt surprise, therefore, when the driving door swung open and a girl in a green dress got out and ran across the road towards her.

'Hi—stop a minute—*please!*'

Gemma stopped as she recognised Julia Moore.

Oh lord, she thought, here we go again! But at least Harn Durrant wasn't here to repeat his performance of this morning.

Julia joined her on the pavement. She really was very beautiful, Gemma thought, with her great violet eyes and her cloud of white-gold hair. But at the moment she looked a wreck. 'I've been waiting for ages,' she gasped. 'Please tell me—isn't Harn in the office?'

Julia looked so awful that Gemma hadn't the heart to brush her off completely. 'He's gone to London,' she said, turning away and beginning to walk down the road. 'Sorry.'

Julia was beside her. 'Oh, don't go—please! I've got to talk to you. Please come and sit in my car for a minute or two.' She grabbed Gemma's arm.

Gemma sighed. She supposed this was part of her new job, and anyway she couldn't help feeling a little sorry for the girl, who was obviously making herself ill over a man who didn't want her.

She said, just as she had said to Derek, 'I don't think I can help, you know.' But she followed Julia across the road and slipped into the passenger seat of the white sports car.

Julia fumbled for a handkerchief and dabbed her eyes. Then she peeped at herself in the driving-mirror. 'I must look terrible,' she said, and Gemma didn't contradict her. She wondered if Harn Durrant reduced all his discarded girl-friends to limp, pathetic wrecks like the girl beside her. She waited, not speaking.

At last Julia stuffed the handkerchief away and sat twisting her fingers together. 'Please tell me,' she burst out desperately, 'are you and Harn having an affair? Oh, don't say anything yet——'

as Gemma's head shot up '—I wouldn't blame you if you are. I know only too well what Harn can be like—how devastating he can be sexually. No girl could resist him.'

I could, Gemma thought firmly. You just watch me. But she still didn't speak.

'I—I know he was kissing you when I went into the office this morning,' Julia stammered, 'but I thought perhaps it was just—you know—men *do* kiss their secretaries, don't they? At least that's what I've been told.' She made a shaky attempt at a laugh. 'Oh dear, I'm not putting this very well.'

She turned her great violet eyes, swimming in tears, on Gemma's face. 'You see, I must know, because it's—it's just about killing me, not being sure. Harn and I have had quarrels before and he's walked out on me, but I've managed to get him to come back. But this time he—he seemed——' She pulled out a handkerchief again and began to sob. 'Oh dear,' she muttered, 'I'm so afraid. If it's really over I think I'll die!'

Gemma began to feel vastly uncomfortable. She was eighteen, but nothing like this had come her way before. 'I'm afraid I can't really give you any advice,' she said calmly. 'Except that no man is worth dying for, and I'm quite sure Harn Durrant isn't. I haven't known him very long, but he seems to me completely lacking in feeling.'

Julia's mouth fell open. 'How can you say that when you——'

Gemma had to avoid the way that question was leading. 'I can say it very well,' she said firmly. 'I've worked with him and I've watched him at work. He's self-centred and arrogant and as hard as nails. Not a man to fall in love with.'

'But—but—he's so wonderful——'

'In bed?' Gemma said dryly. She was putting on a sophisticated act and she wasn't quite sure of her ground, but if she was as yet innocent, she had read books and seen films and she knew what sex was all about—from the outside, at any rate. 'But that's not everything, is it? Certainly not worth dying for.'

'But—but what shall I do?' Julia wailed. Really, the girl was quite pathetically silly, Gemma thought pityingly. Harn had told her to get rid of Julia, but he hadn't told her how. He hadn't told her what a damp, clinging vine Julia was.

A gleam came into her blue eyes. 'I think——' she began, and Julia turned eagerly.

'Yes?'

'I think the best advice is what they tell you when you lose a pet dog. Find another one as soon as possible.'

'Oh!' gasped the girl beside her, outraged. 'Oh, I think that's horrid! You're making fun of me.'

'Not a bit of it,' Gemma said sturdily. 'It's good sound common sense. Now, if you'll excuse me, I really must get home. I hope you feel better about things soon, Miss Moore. He really isn't worth it, you know.'

She slipped out of the car and walked briskly away down the road. Phew! that was gruelling. Harn Durrant certainly had left her with some pieces to pick up, the wretch. Poor Julia, she was no match for a heartless brute like him.

As she walked home Gemma found herself wondering about the kind of girl who *would* be a match for him. It would be interesting to meet her.

CHAPTER FOUR

IAN came to supper on Saturday night, as usual.
Gemma busied herself in the kitchen cooking the
meal, leaving Beth to talk to Ian in the sitting
room, and tell him as much as she chose about the
happenings of the week. Gemma spun out the
cooking as long as she could, but at last she had to
announce that supper was ready.

They all sat down at the pinewood table in the
kitchen alcove and Ian said, 'This *is* a surprise,
Gemma. Beth's been telling me about giving up
her job and you taking it over. It's quite
extraordinary that this should happen just now.'

Why 'just now'? wondered Gemma, as Beth
began to heap macaroni cheese, with grilled
mushrooms and tomatoes, on to Ian's plate. Beth
worried about his living alone and not getting
enough to eat. Ian was everyone's idea of an
artist—tall and very thin, with a neat dark beard
and brilliant black eyes that roamed everywhere
and seemed to be storing away each detail in some
hidden part of his mind. And indeed he did look
rather underfed, Gemma thought, as she glanced
across the table at him and waited for some clue as
to what he meant by that 'just now.'

But Beth spoke first. 'You *do* think it's a good
idea, don't you, Ian?' She sounded almost
pleading. 'It will give Gemma wonderful experience, and she's really keen on the idea of being a
modern super-secretary, aren't you, love?'

Gemma grinned and nodded. Beth was obviously still feeling slightly guilty, but she had not, Gemma guessed, told Ian all the details of her own near-breakdown and Harn Durrant's callous treatment of her. Ian leaned towards her and said earnestly, 'I think it's the best thing that's happened in a long time for all of us. You were due to give up that job, Beth. I've never thought you were cut out to be a secretary. And now you'll be free.' He looked curiously eager.

'Until I've spent all my golden handshake,' Beth laughed. 'Then I'll have to look out for another job. But I don't want to think about that yet. Tell us your news instead.'

Ian looked mysterious, then modest, and finally it came out that he had some very important news indeed. He had just heard that he had won a scholarship which meant that he could spend six months studying and working in Naples.

'Ian! How absolutely wonderful. Naples!' Beth's brown eyes lit with pride and pleasure. 'That's just the beginning of something absolutely terrific for you, I'm sure of it. I always knew you'd get a chance like this one day. Naples!' she repeated, and as she added her own congratulations. Gemma thought she heard a faintly wistful note in her sister's voice.

Of course, talk of Naples occupied the rest of supper-time. Beth had to know every tiny detail and she hung on to Ian's words, wide-eyed. Gemma watched the two of them in silence. They were so well matched, it would be wonderful if they could get married. She sometimes wondered how far their friendship had developed, but Beth was too reserved to talk about a love affair—if indeed there was one, and of course Gemma never asked. She and Beth were from different generations, with different ideas about such things. Not that Beth was stuffy or narrow-minded—but there was a gap between them, as Gemma was sometimes made aware.

When the meal was over she shooed them both out of the kitchen. 'I'll do the washing-up, and then I've promised to go round to the Forsters'. I may go to the flicks with Ann.'

'All right, love. Don't be too late,' Beth added automatically as she led the way back to the sitting room, hardly able to drag her eyes from the tall dark man at her side. Gemma grinned and closed the door behind them. Tactful, that's me, she told herself as she began to pile up the dishes and carry them to the sink.

At half-past nine Monday morning the phone buzzed on Gemma's desk. Mrs Brown's voice said guardedly, 'There's a Miss Vera Knight on the phone, Gemma—wants Mr Durrant. Will you speak to her?'

'Do you know if it's a business call?' Gemma enquired, thinking that forewarned is forearmed.

'I don't imagine so,' Mrs Brown said drily.

'O.K., put her through, please.' Gemma braced herself and cooed into the phone, 'Good morning, this is Mr Durrant's secretary, can I help you?'

A feminine voice, low and sulky, said, 'It's Harn I want to speak to—tell him it's Vee.'

'Sorry,' Gemma said crisply, 'Mr Durrant isn't in the office at present. Is there any message I can give him?'

'He's not there?' The voice sounded suspicious. 'Where is he?'

'I really can't tell you,' Gemma ploughed on patiently. 'He left yesterday. If you'd care to ring again in a few days——'

'I don't believe a word of it.' Miss Vera Knight was forthright and aggressive. 'He's there, I know he is. You're lying!'

'Sorry,' Gemma's voice was icy now, 'you've been misinformed, Miss Knight. Mr Durrant is certainly not in the office and not likely to be here for some days. Good morning.' She replaced the receiver with a click. Another of them, and this one sounded much more disagreeable than poor, pathetic Julia Moore.

She went back to the word-processor manual.

Ten minutes later the phone buzzed again. 'Gemma? Durrant here.' The sudden sound of his voice was so unexpected that Gemma's heart gave a huge lurch. Mrs Brown must have put him straight through without warning her. 'Yes?' she said, and her lips were suddenly dry.

'Speak up, I can't hear you.' His voice came clear and crisp over the wire.

'Yes, Mr Durrant.' Gemma tried again.

'You're all right, are you, Gemma? Not ailing or anything? You seem a trifle woolly.'

Gemma swallowed. 'I'm perfectly well, thank you, Mr Durrant.' This time she sounded fairly normal.

'Good. How are you getting along? Any calls for me?'

'Just one this morning,' she said. 'A Miss Knight.'

She heard his groan from the other end of the

line. 'Oh Gawd, not that one again! What did you tell her?'

'I said you were away, I didn't know where, or how long you'd be.'

'Good girl—that's the stuff, you're doing fine. If she rings again tell her you've heard from me and I've gone to Siberia or the Kalahari Desert.'

Gemma couldn't control a giggle. 'I don't think she'd believe me. As it was she accused me of lying.'

'Never mind, Gemma dear, it's all in a good cause. Now, to business—has Brenda turned up yet?'

Gemma's heart sank. Brenda? Not another of his girl-friends! 'I haven't seen anyone called Brenda. What do I tell *her*?'

'What do you—oh, I see. No, Gemma, you've jumped to a wrong conclusion this time. Brenda is Brenda Johnson and she's coming up from my office here in London to put you in the picture about the word-processor. She should be with you any time now. She's a wizard with the technology— a tremendous girl.' His voice was warm with appreciation. 'Do what she tells you and you'll pick it up in no time.'

'Yes,' said Gemma, glaring at the blank screen beside the typewriter, which seemed to glare back at her superciliously.

'Nothing more to ask about?'

'No, Mr Durrant.' Only a completely crazy desire to ask when he would be coming back. What could she be thinking of?

'Good. 'Bye, then, Gemma.'

'Goodbye, Mr——' Gemma began. But he had rung off.

She sat staring at the receiver in her hand and then replaced it slowly on its cradle. It was annoying and inconvenient that Harn Durrant should have such an effect on her nervous system. Even hearing his voice on the phone made her inside squeeze up. Perhaps when she had been working with him for a little longer familiarity would breed contempt, or at the very least indifference. She sincerely hoped so.

Brenda Johnson arrived an hour later. She breezed in and brought the atmosphere of London and international big business with her.

'Hullo—you're Gemma, are you? Harn Durrant told me all about you.' She grinned in a knowing sort of way that set Gemma wondering exactly *what* Harn had told her. But her smile was friendly too, and Gemma felt relieved as she smiled back. Brenda Johnson was a tremendous girl, Harn had said, and that might have applied to her appearance as much as to her wizardry with a word-processor. She was very tall, very slim, with shining raven-dark hair brushed back with deceptive casualness from an ivory-skinned, attractive face. She wore an easy-fitting black suit and a scarlet silk blouse, and the whole elegant effect was completed by a pair of high black suede boots. There was a wide, chased-gold wedding ring on her left hand.

She glanced round the office with its scratched desks, ancient filing cabinets, ornate ceiling and peeling paintwork. 'Is this where our Harn works? I don't believe it. It's like something out of——'

'A Charles Dickens novel?' Gemma put in, smiling. 'That's what he says. He's having it all rebuilt, I understand.'

'Ah!' Brenda Johnson nodded. 'That figures. A man geared to the twenty-first century, is Mr H. Durrant. And what about you?' She looked Gemma over rather curiously, taking in her neat grey skirt and white striped blouse. 'Do you go along with his streamlined efficiency?'

'Oh yes.' Gemma took Brenda Johnson's jacket as she shrugged it off, and placed it carefully on a hanger on the mahogany coat-stand. 'I'm quite willing to be modernised along with the office.'

Brenda laughed. 'Good for you! We'll get along fine, then. I hate trying to train girls who put up every kind of resistance to being trained, and quite a few of them do.'

She had a nice, gurgly laugh and Gemma decided that she wasn't nearly as frightening as she had feared. In fact, she rather liked her. She glanced towards the desk on which stood the dreaded word-processor. 'Is it very difficult to learn?'

Brenda laughed again. 'Dead easy,' she said reassuringly. 'Come on then, let's get cracking.'

It wasn't exactly dead easy, but it was absolutely fascinating, and two hours and several cups of coffee later Gemma sat back in her chair and let out a huge sigh. 'That's about as much as I can take in one go. How do you feel about lunch, Brenda?'

'A splendid idea! I'm putting up at the Dennington, so we'll go there. My treat—I have my own expense account.'

Gemma looked with frank admiration at the tall elegant girl from London. How would it feel to have a top job and an expense account and travel around in a company car and be able to afford to buy wonderful clothes? she wondered. Would she ever make the grade herself? In the ordinary course of events the answer would be almost certainly No. A young typist with no experience had a long, long way to go. But if she took full advantage of the lucky break she had had, then who knows? she thought with a heady stirring of excitement. It really all depended on whether she could satisfy Harn Durrant.

Brenda stayed two days, during which a feeling of mutual friendliness developed between the two girls, although neither of them volunteered very much in the way of personal information. Brenda merely remarked that her husband was in the Navy and that she was a grass widow much of the time, although she didn't get bored, with such an interesting job to devote herself to. Gemma spoke of Beth and her hopes of one day being an artist, but said nothing about her having worked for Durrants for many years. Most of the time, however, was devoted to work on the word-processor, and at the end of the four sessions Brenda expressed herself very satisfied with Gemma's progress.

'I'd planned to give you two more sessions,' she said, when Gemma went down to the car-park to see her off, 'but it would be a waste of time for both of us. You've picked it up very quickly and the thing to do now is to practise and practise and then have another session or two in a few weeks. I usually reckon that it takes a month or six weeks to become absolutely at home with a word-processor, but you're bright, Gemma, and I feel you won't need as long as that. You've got the manual to refer to, and if you get stuck I'll be on the phone and ready to help you at any time. If I'm not in the office myself they'll put you on to one of the other girls. And—of course—you'll have the great Mr Harn Durrant here to refer to. There's nothing he doesn't know about computers of all kinds.' Her lips twisted in a little ironic smile as they always did when she spoke of Harn. Gemma wished she knew why.

She said quickly, 'Oh, I wouldn't want to ask him for help. That would be a confession of failure.' She realised suddenly how much she wanted to impress Harn Durrant with her expertise when he returned.

Brenda glanced sideways at her. 'How long have you been working for Harn Durrant?'

'Only a very short time.' Gemma hadn't said anything about the very odd way that she had acquired the job, and Harn had evidently not mentioned the circumstances to Brenda before she came.

Brenda nodded slowly. 'He takes a bit of getting used to. He expects a lot.'

'Oh yes, I realise that. He's got a fabulous brain, I've learned that already.'

Brenda's lips twitched. 'It's not only his brain that's fabulous. Right, Gemma, I expect you'll learn as you go. But you're very young and very pretty, if that doesn't sound patronising from an old married woman, and Harn Durrant's a danger to any girl's peace of mind, so just watch your step with him, that's all. Cheerio, Gemma, it's been nice meeting you, I hope we'll see each other again.' She climbed into her smart white Mini and reversed neatly out of the yard with a hand raised in salute.

Gemma climbed slowly back up the wooden stairs to the office. Everything was warning her to consider Harn Durrant merely as her employer, a man who could help her to a successful career, and not to allow herself to think of him in any other way. But the memory of that moment he had held her in his arms and kissed her so expertly and so lingeringly, and the memory of his voice on the tape '——love me? I adore you,' kept coming back to make her heart throb unevenly.

She wasn't falling in love with the man, she was merely getting a king-size crush on him, she assured herself. An adolescent crush—rather late, perhaps, something she should have had, but hadn't, at school when all the other girls were falling madly for pop stars. She would have to get over it and not make a fool of herself. She would pattern herself on Brenda Johnson—cool, competent, a thoroughly modern girl who could conduct her own life on intelligent lines and not get in a messy emotional tizz about any man.

Having come to this sensible resolve, Gemma went back to the word-processor, which was still switched on and buzzing away on her desk. It looked almost like an old friend now, but somehow the two little red lights on the cabinet seemed to her ominously like danger signals.

For the next few days Gemma worked against time, determined to be expert on the word-processor by the time Harn returned. He phoned briefly each day but she had little to report. What correspondence there was could easily wait until he could deal with it himself, and Mrs Brown and Ted, between them, were looking after the ordering and selling side. He didn't say how long he would be away, and she didn't enquire. He sounded detached and almost uninterested, and she guessed that the London business was absorbing all his energies. In short, the phone conversations were unsatisfactory and left Gemma feeling vaguely depressed when she put down the receiver. It was as if Harn had left this small backwater and was now engaged in his really important work in London.

It wasn't much better at home. Beth was curiously preoccupied, and although she asked Gemma each day how she was getting on at the office, it was plain that her thoughts were elsewhere. With Ian, Gemma guessed, and that was only natural. Ian would soon be going away for six months at least, and that would leave a great gap in Beth's life. Gemma tried several times to interest her in the idea of art school, with no success. 'It's much too late,' Beth said firmly, and that was that. She cleaned the house and did the shopping and cooking and went about looking lost and unhappy. Gemma began to wonder uneasily if she had done the right thing, after all, in taking on the job in Beth's place. Perhaps Beth should have been left to work out her notice and then try for a secretarial job elsewhere.

On Friday Derek Underhill came into the office. 'Hullo, Gemma, boss not back yet?'

Gemma smiled at him, and—because she was feeling a bit lonely and depressed—perhaps the smile was a little more pleased and welcoming than she intended it to be. A broad grin spread across Derek's thin face. 'Hey, I believe you're really glad to see me!'

'Of course I am,' she grinned back. 'How's the work going?'

'Quite well, I hope.' He patted the portfolio under his arm lovingly and rested it against the leg of Harn's desk, and came down the office towards Gemma. 'I'm going to dazzle your perfectionist boss with the excellence of my ideas. When's he due back, by the way?'

Gemma shook her head. 'I haven't heard yet. Not this week, evidently.'

Derek studied her face thoughtfully for a moment. 'Well, don't let that get you down. You have a willing substitute here.' He patted his chest. 'How about coming out to lunch with me?'

Gemma hesitated, glancing up at the clock. 'It isn't quite my time yet. I've got a couple more letters to do. Perhaps another day, Derek.'

'I can wait for you,' he said. 'Do come.' He paused. 'No strings attached, you know.'

She sighed resignedly. 'O.K., Derek. Ten minutes, then.' She turned back to the word-processor.

Derek came round to her side of the desk. 'I *say*! You've got one of those space-age contraptions, have you? May I look, or does it bite?'

'Only sometimes,' laughed Gemma, and proceeded to demonstrate, while Derek looked on admiringly.

'You're a ruddy marvel, Gemma,' he said when the first letter appeared on the screen. 'When did you learn to work this gadget?'

'Only this week—I've been taking lessons.' She turned and looked up at him, pleased with his admiration, her lips parted in a smile.

She heard his quick intake of breath. He was leaning over her shoulder and their faces were very close together. 'Don't look at me like that, Gemma, or——'

'Or what?' enquired a cold, steely voice from the open doorway. 'If you have any ideas about seducing my secretary, Underhill, you'd better forget them.'

Derek straightened up, his cheeks flushing dully as Harn Durrant came into the office, looking like thunder. Gemma was struck completely dumb.

'I assure you, Mr Durrant,' Derek said with some dignity, 'that seducing pretty girls isn't one of my habits. I merely admiring her skill with this new instrument she seems so expert at handling.'

Harn snapped, 'Admiring more than her skill, I should imagine. Never mind, let it go.' He strode across to his desk without a glance at Gemma. She might have been part of the office furniture. She had a sick feeling inside. She had planned that Harn would find everything going smoothly on his return, and it could hardly have turned out to be worse. It occurred to her that he had climbed the wooden stairs very quietly. Had Mrs Brown told him that Derek was here? Had he thought he might catch her wasting office time in a flirtation?

Derek followed Harn across the office and picked up his portfolio. 'I came in in the hope of seeing you, Mr Durrant,' he said in a businesslike tone, ignoring the cynical lift of Harn Durrant's dark brows. 'I have two alternative plans here, ready for your decision.' He took out the plans and laid them on the desk.

Harn glanced at them indifferently. 'O.K., leave them with me.' He pushed the plans out of the way and picked up the unopened post that was marked 'Personal' and which Gemma hadn't dealt with.

Derek hovered uncertainly, with a glance across at Gemma, which she pretended not to notice.

Harn paid him no further attention, finished reading his letter, and then glanced in Gemma's direction. 'Come along, Gemma, we'll go out and have lunch. I have things to discuss with you.'

Gemma looked helplessly at Derek, hoping that he would understand that their lunch date was well and truly cancelled, and why.

After a moment or two of silence he did just that. 'Good morning, then, Mr Durrant. I'll expect to hear from you.'

Harn raised his head from the letter he was reading, glanced vaguely at Derek as if he had never seen him before, then murmured indifferently, 'Oh—oh yes, probably.'

Derek pulled a face of utter frustration, and with an angry shrug, left the office. Gemma felt angry too, on his behalf. It was really intolerable, the way this man Harn Durrant treated the people who worked for him. She began very deliberately to go through the procedure of signing off the word-processor, taking out the discs and putting them carefully in their cardboard covers.

'Come along, hurry up!' Harn's voice was impatient and irritable but she didn't allow it to distract her concentration. It was, she knew, fatally easy to damage the discs if you were careless.

She replaced the discs in their box and snapped it closed, switched off the machine, and only then did she join him at the other end of the office.

'You took your time,' he said nastily. He really did seem to be in a vile humour.

She smiled coolly, ignoring his rudeness. 'I'm

ready now,' she said. She saw the dark look he gave her as she led the way out of the office and down the stairs.

They lunched at the Dennington Hotel at the same table in the corner that they had had before. Gemma had no appetite; she felt that food would choke her. 'Just soup, please, and a roll.'

Harn took a tray to the chef's table and brought it back with her soup and a loaded plate of cold meats and salad for himself. 'I didn't stop to eat breakfast,' he explained shortly.

His plate was half empty before he spoke again, but Gemma had only managed to spoon a little soup down and was toying with her roll. 'Now then, Gemma, tell me what's been going on in my absence. And I don't want to hear about any funny business between you and Derek Architect Underhill either.'

Indignation made her simmer inside, but she controlled it and said coldly, 'There was no funny business. He came in with new plans, that's all, only minutes before you crept up the stairs.'

'Ha, you thought I was snooping, did you?'

She met his ironical gaze squarely. 'Weren't you?'

'Don't be childish, Gemma. I don't care what you get up to with young Underhill, just so long as you don't waste office time. And for the record,' he added with a grin, 'I've bought myself a new pair of shoes—rubber-soled.' The eyelashes lowered themselves. 'So now you won't know where I am, will you?'

Gemma smiled reluctantly. He could make her look a fool with no effort at all. She was no match for him.

His expression changed; it was back to business again. 'Well, what's the report? How did you get along with Brenda? I saw her briefly when she came back and she said you were very quick on the uptake. Did you enjoy your training?'

Gemma went pink with pleasure. 'Oh, yes, very much. Brenda was marvellous, as you promised she would be, and very patient with me. I'm beginning to feel at home with the word-processor by now. It would be quite a bore to go back to an ordinary typewriter.'

Harn was looking at her oddly. 'That's my Gemma,' he said. And then, 'Do you know your eyes change colour when you're excited—they sparkle like blue diamonds. It's quite an interesting phenomenon, one that I've never seen before.'

Gemma blinked. 'Really?' she murmured dazedly. The man's moods changed like quicksilver. You didn't know where you were with him from one moment to the next.

Rather to her disappointment he didn't pursue the subject. 'I'm glad you're getting expert with the technology.' he said. 'That will be very useful. What about the day-to-day business? Anything unusual turn up?'

She shook her head. 'I don't think so. Mrs Brown was busy with the books and Ted was stocktaking. I typed some of her letters so that Ann could help in the shop. I think they got on pretty well with the stocktaking. There were one or two phone calls for you, but none of them seemed urgent. I've made notes of them for you to deal with.'

'Business calls?'

'Well—er—yes, most of them.'

'Tell me about the ones that weren't.'

'There was this Miss Knight kept ringing up. She wouldn't believe you weren't in the office. I had to be very firm with her.'

He smiled. 'That I should like to have heard.'

She said defensively. 'I can be firm if I want to, you know. I dealt with Miss Moore for you too.'

'Julia? She turned up again? I was afraid she might. Unlike Vera, who has a job to hold down, Julia's time is her own and Daddy's money makes her a very spoilt girl. What did she want?'

'She wanted you, of course, but when I told her you were away she——' she broke off.

'Yes?' he prompted quite gently.

Gemma swallowed and continued valiantly, 'She tried to find out if you—if you and I were——'

'Sleeping together?' he drawled, and she nodded mutely.

'Oh dear,' he said, grimacing. 'I fear I've put you in a false position, Gemma. Please accept my humble apology. I'm very sorry.'

Her anger flared suddenly as she caught his look of suppressed amusement. 'I don't think you *are* sorry,' she said hotly. 'Neither can I imagine you being humble.'

He pursed his lips and nodded judicially. 'You're wrong, Gemma, I can be very humble when I'm asking for something I want badly.' His lashes lowered and his eyes held hers in a long, long look that made her shake inside.

But she managed to hang on to her annoyance, trying to ignore the way her heart was thumping against her ribs. 'I'd like to get this clear, Mr Durrant, before I go on working for you. You did indeed put me in a false position when Miss

Moore came into the office the other day and you—and you——' her mouth dried up and she gulped humiliatingly.

'Yes?' he enquired with a mocking smile. 'I what?'

'You k-kissed me,' Gemma muttered, pink with embarrassment.

He leaned back in his chair, studying her face. 'So I did, and very pleasant it was too. You're eminently kissable, Gemma Lawson, as I'm sure you've been told many times before in your young life.'

She forgot he was her boss and she a paid employee. 'Oh, shut up!' she burst out desperately, with a quick glance round the room at the other tables, most of which were fortunately empty. 'Let me say what I want to say. I think I know now why you engaged me—one of the reasons that you didn't tell me when I asked you. I think you want to give the impression that we're—we're having an affair. I think you want me as a—a kind of—of hedge to keep away your girl-friends when they get too demanding, or won't take no for an answer.'

There was a long silence and she crumbled her roll into small pieces and kept her eyes on her plate.

At last he said, 'So that's what your clever little brain has come up with, is it?'

'Yes.' She met his look defiantly now. She had started this and she was going to see it through. 'And there's no need to be sarcastic. I think you're just *using* me, and I object to being used. I was prepared to stand in for Beth because it suited me to do so, but I'm not prepared to stay and work as your secretary if it means that people think I'm—

I'm your mistress. Which,' she ended triumphantly, 'I'd rather die than be!'

He smiled hatefully. 'Very concisely put, Miss Lawson. Though your grammar is a bit shaky, don't you think?'

She glared at him, 'Oh, you, you——' she gasped, close to tears.

He regarded her for a moment, then he leaned across the table and covered her hands with his own strong ones, his long firm fingers winding themselves round hers. 'Poor little Gemma,' he murmured. 'It's a shame to tease you, you're so very young, but you rise to the bait so deliciously, and I must admit that a girl who can still blush is quite a novelty these days. But to return to your accusation, which I emphatically deny. No, I didn't engage you to choke off my too-demanding women friends. Normally I can do my own choking off without any help.'

She looked at him, at the hard, almost haughty lines of his face, heard the arrogant note in his voice, and thought she could well believe that.

'I really am sorry,' he went on, 'that the little episode with Julia upset you. When I kissed you I acted on impulse, which is a thing I rarely do, and it was entirely because I wanted to save myself— and you—from the scene that I knew was brewing, and that I hadn't time to deal with if I wanted to catch my train to London. And that's all there was to it.'

But it wasn't all, Gemma remembered only too well. That first kiss had been followed by another after Julia had left, one that Julia hadn't witnessed, so his explanation didn't hold water.

'There—I've apologised,' he said gently. 'Satisfied?'

Gemma wasn't satisfied. She didn't understand Harn Durrant and she didn't trust him. Common sense, and something more—a feeling that she was out of her depth with this man—told her that she ought to say no, she wasn't satisfied. That she wasn't prepared to carry on with the job, and that he must look for someone else to take Beth's place. But some stronger urge that she didn't understand made it impossible for her to say the words.

'I—I suppose so,' she muttered, and felt his fingers on hers in a hard pressure. 'Good,' he said, and he looked really pleased, although probably he was just relieved that he wouldn't have to start looking for another secretary, Gemma assured herself.

'Just as a matter of interest, though,' he quizzed her, 'how did you manage to get rid of Julia?'

Here was an opportunity to score a point. 'I pointed out that you weren't worth breaking her heart over,' she said coolly. 'And I advised her to do what they tell you to do when you lose a pet dog—go out and get another one as soon as you can.'

His head jerked back, mimicking a blow received on the jaw. Then he roared with laughter. 'Oh, Gemma, you're superb! What should I do without you?'

Reluctantly she smiled. Then they were both laughing together and suddenly everything was different. As he left her to procure coffee Gemma watched his tall figure moving easily across the long room, between the tables, to the white-clothed service counter, and her doubts and fears began to drift away. He looked every inch a top executive and she could envisage a future where she worked intimately with him, as a personal secretary should, understanding him, making allowances for him, not taking offence when he was irritable, defending him against silly people who tried to encroach on his time and attention.

She was brought back from this rosy dream as he placed her coffee on the table before her and said, 'And now, let me explain what I've got in mind for the immediate future. I shall accept one of young Underhill's plans for the new building here and tell him to get on with it immediately. As I won't have an office until it's finished I've decided to scrap all the office furniture, move anything essential—the files and so on—down to Mrs Brown's department, and leave that good lady in charge until the building work is completed. I suppose it will take a matter of months. Meanwhile I shall return to London.'

'Oh!' she breathed, and her stomach felt as if she had suddenly gone down in a lift. The deadly feeling of disappointment took her by surprise. Not to see him for months!

He was watching her face closely. 'I shall, of course, want you to come to London with me,' he said.

That took her breath away and she gaped at him. 'Come to London—with you?' she repeated stupidly.

He smiled faintly. 'Don't make it sound like an improper suggestion! I should require your services only as a secretary, in spite of all your nasty suspicions.' He became serious. 'I realise this is a bit of a surprise to you, Gemma. You're very young and this is your first job, but—as I said once before—I think you're a girl who is at home in the modern world, and the modern world is full of challenges. The woman who's been working as my secretary in London is leaving in a couple of weeks to have a baby, and I shall need a replacement. From what I've seen of your work and heard of the way you've already come to terms with the technology, I think you'll do very well.'

'But—but London——' Gemma stammered. All her plans about being cool and collected were in ruins after this surprise attack on them. 'I don't know London at all. I wouldn't have anywhere to live or anything.'

'That's arranged,' he said crisply. 'Brenda Johnson is willing to give you a room in her flat for the time being. Her husband is away serving in the Far East and I think she would be quite glad of some company.'

'I don't know,' Gemma said doubtfully, thinking of what Beth would say; thinking too of leaving Beth alone when Ian was off to Naples. 'May I think it over?'

'If you must,' he said, suddenly cold. 'Let me know tomorrow morning at the latest.' He tossed down the remainder of his coffee and got to his feet. 'Are you ready now? We'll get the removal work started.'

Oh dear, Gemma thought in utter confusion, as she followed him out to his car, the only bonus in all this is that apparently Derek will get the job he so much wants.

The afternoon passed in a hectic rush of activity. Summoned by telephone, Derek Underhill appeared, looking apprehensive. After a very brief conference Harn accepted one of his two new plans in its entirety. 'Get cracking straight away, will you? We shan't need planning permission for this work, you said? You've got your builders lined up? Good. I shall leave the whole project in your hands, then—you'll be accountable to me. I shall be in London while the work is going on and I'll phone occasionally for a progress report. Is all that clear?'

'You'll be in London?' Derek repeated with a glance towards Gemma, who was piling up files on her desk, and Harn smiled grimly.

'Yes, and my secretary will be coming with me.'

Derek Underhill flushed and said nothing. Gemma almost yelled across the office that she hadn't made up her mind yet, but thought better of it. A cool modern girl wouldn't behave like that.

She carried the files down to Mrs Brown's office and was there for some time, rearranging them to that lady's satisfaction. When she got back upstairs Derek had gone and Harn was poring over his desk looking totally absorbed in his work.

'That's all for today, Gemma,' he said, without looking up. 'You can go home now.'

Feeling decidedly weak at the knees, Gemma went.

Beth was drooping listlessly over the cooker stirring something in a pan when Gemma opened the door half an hour later, but she turned and summoned a smile. 'Hullo, love, how's things?'

'Chaotic!' Gemma pulled a face and collapsed into the old wicker chair by the kitchen stove. 'Mr Durrant turned up today unexpectedly and after that the place was in a ferment. He's having the whole office re-vamped and modernised—I told you. And now he's decided on the plans, he's going back to work in London while the builders are in.'

Beth pushed the pan aside, and came across the kitchen. 'So your job will come to an end so soon? Poor old Gem, what a shame. You were really beginning to enjoy all that horrid mechanical stuff, weren't you?'

Gemma took a deep breath. 'He wants me to go to London with him,' she said, and added hastily, 'His secretary there is leaving. He seems to take it for granted that I'll go. He's even arranged for me to live with Brenda Johnson—the girl who came for my training—for the time being.'

Beth said slowly, 'And do you want to go?'

'I don't know,' Gemma confessed. 'I don't want to leave you on your own, Beth. Oh, I know what you'll say—that I mustn't miss a chance like this because of you, but——'

Beth said, 'But do you *want* to go?' Her voice sounded odd.

Gemma considered in silence, then said haltingly, 'Well, I suppose—other things being equal—yes, I think it might be quite an experience. London, the hub of the country's business—just the place for an ambitious young secretary!' She pulled a face. 'But I'm not going to leave you on your own, Beth, now that Ian's going away, and that's final. Heavens, it's not as important to me as all that.' *But it is,* something inside her whispered traitorously, *it's terribly important.* And that had nothing to do with being an ambitious young secretary, either.

She realised that Beth's shoulder's were shaking
with laughter. 'We are a couple of mugs,' she
spluttered at last, wiping her eyes. 'Here are you,
thinking of missing a wonderful opportunity of
going to London because of me, and here am I
turning down a chance to go to Naples because I
couldn't think of leaving you on your own here.
Oh, Gem darling, we've both been pretty idiotic!'

'Naples—you?' Gemma goggled.

'Um,' Beth nodded, her brown eyes shining. 'Ian
wants me to go along with him, and I could use
my hand-out from Durrants to do it. I could
probably get a job there—teaching English,
perhaps, or something. Washing up in a restaurant
even. I'd do anything to get to Naples. He——'
she hesitated, then flushed. 'He wants us to get
married later on, Gem, but——'

Gemma flung her arms round Beth's neck and
hugged her tightly. 'It's the most wonderful thing
that's ever happened! I couldn't have wished for
anything nicer. Ian's a pet, and I'm sure you'll be
so happy together. Oh, Beth love, let's start
making plans straight away. And when we've had
supper you must go and see Ian and tell him Yes.'

'But——' Beth began again, but Gemma put a
hand over her mouth.

'No buts, that's what's going to happen.' And
Beth laughed shakily and agreed.

'And you'll go to London? You'll enjoy it?
You're *sure*?'

'Yes, I'll go to London,' Gemma echoed. 'I'll
enjoy it, I'm sure.'

But when she had seen Beth off, bubbling with
excitement on her way to tell Ian the good news,
Gemma sat down and drank the last cup of coffee

in the pot and tried to quieten her tingling nerves. This was her chance to become a cool, competent London girl like Brenda. A thoroughly modern girl. She couldn't miss the challenge now. But— enjoy it? She wasn't sure about that at all.

In fact, remembering Harn Durrant's dark eyes and the way they had regarded her across the table, she felt she would never be sure about anything again, least of all about his plans for her. That look had frightened and excited her. She was taking a huge leap in the dark, and butterflies were lurching wildly about her stomach as she contemplated the immediate future.

CHAPTER FIVE

GEMMA arrived at the office next morning to find it stripped almost bare. Two workmen in blue overalls were removing the large, shabby desk where Harn had worked. Her own desk had disappeared, as had the chairs and the filing cabinets and the curly mahogany coat-stand. And of course the word-processor was nowhere to be seen.

Harn glanced over his shoulder at her from where he was standing at the window, reading a letter. 'Well,' he enquired brusquely, 'have you made up your mind if you can face the challenge of the Big Bad City?'

She hated it when he was sarcastic. 'If you want me to work in London, Mr Durrant, I'm prepared to do so,' she said calmly.

'Thank you for that generous concession.' The tone was still ironic, but she thought she detected a hint of triumph in his voice. He wasn't a man who liked to be refused anything.

He folded the letter and put it back in its envelope. The paper and the envelope were a pale mauve colour and Gemma thought she detected a faint perfume in the air, which certainly didn't come from Harn Durrant.

'Let's make a few plans, then,' he said. 'Obviously there will be no more work done here today, so I suggest you go back home and do some packing and I'll drive you up to Town this afternoon and park you with Brenda. She'll be expecting you. Run along now, and I'll pick you up at your home around five.' He pulled out a notebook and pencil. 'What's the address?'

Gemma felt as if the ground was being cut away under her feet and there was a deep abyss in front of her, but she pulled herself together sufficiently to say, 'I'm not sure I'll be ready by five. And I'd much prefer it if you didn't call at my home.'

He frowned. 'Why—to both questions?'

'Well, I—I haven't really got enough clothes suitable for working in London. I was going to buy some first.'

'That's easily settled. You can do your shopping when you get there. Much more choice, and Brenda knows the best shops; she'll be able to help you. Why don't you want me to pick you up at your home?'

Heavens, the man was insensitive! She said coldly, 'Because I doubt if my sister would care to see you.'

He looked faintly amused. 'Really? Is she still bearing a grudge?'

Gemma nearly blurted out, 'No—but I'm bearing a grudge on her behalf.' Instead she said quietly, 'I think it would be better if I took a taxi. I could meet you wherever you say.'

Harn shrugged without interest. 'Okay, if that's what you want. You can come to my flat.' He scribbled down the address, tore the leaf from his notebook and handed it to her. 'Don't be late,' he added, and it seemed like the parting shot in a battle.

Gemma would rather have died than be late. The taxi deposited her outside a block of custom-built flats at the expensive end of the town on the dot of five. Harn was standing beside his car in the private car-park and he stepped forward and paid her driver before she had a chance to get out her purse. He loaded her bags on to the back seat of the Mercedes, beside his own.

'Hop in,' he said, and slid into the driving seat, leaning across to open the passenger door for her. Gemma almost fell into the seat beside him. She had the impression that if she didn't get in quickly he might drive away without her—a man in a hurry, that was Harn Durrant.

He didn't seem inclined to talk, and Gemma leaned back against the soft pale leather of the seat and tried to relax, but it wasn't easy. She was tense as she kept remembering Beth's final words.

'Your life's your own now, Gem,' Beth had said as they stood on the doorstep of their home, waiting for the taxi. 'You'll make a success of things, I know you will. I'm just sorry——' She broke off, biting her lip.

'Sorry about?'

'I've got to say it, darling. I'm sorry it's Harn

Durrant that you're going to London with. He's not right for you.'

'Beth!' Gemma laughed, squeezing her sister's arm. 'I'm going to work for the man, not marry him!'

Beth joined in the laughter. 'I should hope not indeed! I don't fancy that man as a brother-in-law.'

The taxi drew up then, and they hugged each other and Gemma promised to send her address as soon as she knew it, and Beth promised to write often from Naples and send some picture postcards, and they were both very conscious that this parting was the end of a phase in both their lives, and neither of them was very far from tears.

Now Gemma glanced sideways at the strong, arrogant profile of the man beside her and a wriggle of fear caught at her inside. Beth had said, 'Your life is your own,' but it seemed to Gemma that Harn Durrant had taken her life into his unfeeling charge and was doing just what he liked with her. Everything he had asked (demanded?) of her so far she had meekly agreed to.

They had joined the motorway now and Harn flicked her a glance as he eased the Mercedes into the middle lane. 'You're not alarmed by a touch of speed, I hope?'

'I don't know,' Gemma confessed. 'I've never driven in a car like this before.'

'We must initiate you, then,' he smiled with a glance in the driving-mirror. The car moved to the fast lane, purring like a great cat, and streaked along, flashing past every other vehicle on the road. Gemma's eyes went to the speedometer. Ninety—ninety-five—just on a hundred miles an hour. She didn't know very much about speed limits but guessed that Harn was undoubtedly exceeding it, whatever it was. His fingers were firm but not tense on the driving-wheel and he sat back in his seat without a sign of strain. He was enjoying this. After a couple of minutes Gemma found that she was enjoying it too. It was as if everything in her were singing, and she felt all bubbly as you were supposed to do when you drank champagne. That was another experience she had never had. So many exciting things loomed ahead that she felt quite dizzy with the prospect, and already her fears and regrets about leaving home were getting more feeble.

Nearer to London they were in the heavy traffic and Harn had perforce to reduce his speed to a more moderate one. 'Well, did you enjoy it?' he asked.

'Oh, it was wonderful!' she breathed ecstatically. 'I haven't been so thrilled since I went on the big dipper on a day trip to Blackpool!'

He laughed aloud. 'What a child you are, Gemma! I fear I'm cradle-snatching, luring you away from home.'

All her pleasure evaporated. That had been a stupid thing to say, she scolded herself. 'I learn fast,' she said stiffly, and that observation wasn't much better, because he was still laughing as they left the motorway and he had to concentrate on London's crowded streets.

The clock on the dashboard said it was a quarter past six. Gemma supposed this was the rush-hour, and it certainly seemed like it. She was fascinated and impressed by the way Harn Durrant handled the big car, weaving in and out

of the traffic, over bridges and through under-
passes. At last he turned into the wide forecourt
of a large modern complex of buildings and
backed the car skilfully into one of the few empty
parking spaces.

'I'll take you up and see you installed,' he said,
and hauled Gemma's cases out of the back of the
car.

There was a long strip of name-plates beside
the front door and he pressed one of the
bell-pushes. When there was no reply he said,
'Brenda's not back yet, evidently. We'll let
ourselves in.' He took out a key and opened the
door and carried the luggage across a hall that
looked to Gemma more like the lounge of a
hotel than the entrance to a block of flats—very
plushy, with matt white paint and scarlet carpet
and tubs of flowering plants. Harn pressed a
button for the lift and when it came it was so
small that Gemma couldn't see how they would
both fit in, as well as her two large cases. But fit
in they did, and it meant that she was pressed
against Harn's side and couldn't move unless she
climbed up on one of the cases.

She was much closer to him than she had been
in the car and suddenly she felt breathless as she
became aware that the softness of her breast was
intimately in contact with a point somewhere in
the middle of his ribs. He reached round her to
press the third-floor button, and as the lift started
to ascend silently his hand came down and
rested on her shoulder. She didn't dare look up,
for his face was only inches above hers; she could
feel the warmth of his breath stirring her hair. And
it was not only her hair that was stirred; the

emotions that were wakening and flooding her body were terrifyingly new and disturbing.

She edged away a fraction and felt his hand tighten on her shoulder. 'Rather a squash in here,' he murmured just above her head. 'I always thought the lifts here were specially designed with lovers in mind.' His voice was light and amused, and when the gates opened he held her a trifle closer for a moment before she could step out. Her knees felt distinctly wobbly and her inside was churning. This was dreadful! She must somehow manage to keep a distance between herself and Harn Durrant in the future. That shouldn't be too difficult once the office work got under way.

Brenda's door was one of three on the fifth floor. Harn fitted another key into the lock and pushed the door open. Gemma wondered if he had a key to the living quarters of all his senior staff or if——

'In case you're thinking darkly that I'm very much at home here, having a key and letting myself in,' he said as he dumped her cases in the hall, 'Brenda and I work very closely together and it suits me to be able to use her flat for our consultations at times. There's nothing more to it than that, so you can put any dark suspicions out of your mind.'

Gemma faltered, 'I wasn't—I didn't think——'

He leaned his back against the front door to close it and smiled down at her, his long dark lashes brushing his cheeks. 'Oh yes, you did,' he said. 'You think I'm a playboy, don't you, Gemma? You've judged me already and are wondering whether you're safe with me.' His smile widened. 'I have news for you, young lady. When you look at me like that, with those blue diamond eyes of yours—you're *not*! Now come along in, and we'll raid Brenda's cupboard and see if she has any drinks to revive us.'

He led the way into a spacious living-room, and at once Gemma sensed Brenda's personality at work here, in the arrangement of coffee-coloured lounge chairs and sofas round a central low, square, glass-topped table. One pale-wood fitment ran the whole length of one side of the room, with shelves and compartments to hold books, records, hi-fi, a TV set, flowers, photographs. All the oddments that were scattered so haphazardly around at home were here arranged methodically but attractively.

Gemma stood looking around, admiring everything, and Harn said, 'Nice room, don't you think?'

'It's lovely,' said Gemma. 'Really lovely.' She walked across to the big picture window and stood looking down at a breathtaking view across the river. The sun had set, but the afterglow still lingered over the water, touching it with pinks and golds.

Harn had come up behind her and stood resting one hand against the window-frame, pointing out landmarks. 'That's Tower Bridge, of course. You're near the Tower of London here,' he added, gently mocking, 'so you'll feel quite safe and protected.' His other hand came down to rest on her shoulder.

Gemma forgot the room and the view and everything except the closeness of this man who had the power to turn her bones to water. She tried to make herself pull away from under his enclosing arm, but her legs refused to move.

'What a little thing you are,' he murmured. 'My hands could almost meet round you.' His hands slipped down her body, resting momentarily against her breasts as they did so, and enclosed her waist, drawing her back against him.

Strangely, it didn't surprise her; it seemed absolutely natural that she should lean back, resting her cheek against the smooth stuff of his jacket. It was as if she had done it a hundred times before.

'Not so very little,' she laughed shakily. 'Look, my head reaches up way beyond your shoulder.' Keep it light, she thought desperately.

'So it does,' he said. 'Just the right height for me.' He rubbed his mouth against her hair.

This was fooling, of course, Gemma reminded herself, just the merest of flirtations. Perhaps not routine behaviour with his secretary, but then their relationship had been somewhat out of the ordinary right from the start.

'Just the right height,' Harn repeated, and he turned her round to face him, his hands still holding her waist. Her head was lowered; she didn't dare to look up at him, but now he removed one hand and tipped her chin up with his forefinger. Their eyes met and Gemma's senses reeled. It was just like it had been before, in the office. The space between them seemed to vibrate. She knew he was going to kiss her and the urgency of her need for it to happen was almost shocking. She began to tremble and her lips parted weakly, invitingly.

'You little witch,' he muttered, and pulled her strongly against him, forcing her head back as his mouth came down on hers, passionate, demanding.

Shivers of delight passed through her as she strained against him, her hands reaching up behind his head to tangle in his thick dark hair. She was lost, floating in deep water, great waves washing over her, as she responded to his probing kiss. His hands slipped down from her waist, pressing her hard against him in one final convulsive movement, and then he pushed her away, not very gently.

'That's enough of that,' he muttered, and walked from the window, leaving her feeling lost and ready to burst into tears. 'I'm sorry, Gemma, I should never have started it. You're too damned tempting altogether, and I'm only too human.' He looked across the room at her broodingly. 'Perhaps I shouldn't have taken you on, much less brought you to London. I've never gone in for cradle-snatching.'

Gemma stood where he had left her, humiliation burning through her. She had been utterly shameful, responding to him as if she were starving for sex. She had never behaved like this before with any other man, never felt this overwhelming need. She should have stayed safely within her own league, with a nice, uncomplicated young man like Derek perhaps, not tangled with a worldly, sophisticated type like Harn Durrant.

He was opening a cupboard door, taking out glasses and bottles. She watched his shoulders, straining against the fine stuff of his jacket as he leaned forward, and she shrank inwardly from the threatening strength of the man. For a moment she felt lost, a prey to fear and dismay. Then, like flipping a coin, the other side of the situation came to her. *You knew this would happen, so don't fool*

yourself you didn't. Now you've got to deal with it.
It was a challenge, the biggest challenge of her life
so far. Much more difficult than learning to use a
word-processor, she thought, with a smothered
little laugh.

Harn turned at the sound. 'What's funny?' he
asked, and she knew from his face that he had
been expecting her to be dissolved in tears. That
was how he seemed to affect most women. But she
wasn't most women, Gemma assured herself
firmly. She was Gemma Lawson and she had come
to London to learn about growing up—amongst
other things. She would regard the scene that had
just passed as part of the process. And if Harn
Durrant thought that he was in danger of having
another hysterical female on his hands he could
think again.

She heard herself say in a cool, composed little
voice, 'I'd like a bitter lemon, please, if there's one
there.'

Harn Durrant's face never gave away much of
what he was thinking. Apart from a slight lift of
his brows it showed nothing now. He took out a
bottle and poured her the drink, placing it on the
glass-topped table. Then he poured a drink of
some sort for himself—whisky, it looked like—and
they sat down opposite each other like two
opponents in a debate, and drank in silence.

'Thank you, that was lovely.' Gemma put down
her glass, grateful for the cold, stinging liquid that
bit at her dry throat.

He tossed down his own drink and began
resolutely, 'Gemma, I think perhaps it would be
wiser if you——'

'Please.' She lifted a hand and surprisingly he

stopped. 'If you were thinking of giving me the sack because of that utterly unimportant little episode that has just happened, then forget it. It makes absolutely no difference to the fact that I've come up to London to work for you. I won't hold it against you that you're a man and I——' she pulled a wry face '—I seem to be a woman. We just won't let it happen again, that's all. Agreed?'

He cradled his glass between his hands and frowned at her across the table. 'You're a cool child, Gemma. Where did you learn all that wisdom?'

She said as she had said before, 'Intuition, I suppose.'

He nodded thoughtfully, his eyes fixed on her small, serious face. 'That's the thing women are supposed to have and men to be short on.' He added wryly, 'You'll have to teach me, Gemma.'

There was the sound of a key in the lock and Brenda walked into the room. She wore a snappy black outfit with floating emerald green round the neck and she looked as if she had just stepped out of a beauty parlour instead of having been working all day. 'Hullo, both of you, you got ahead of me. Jennifer had a bit of trouble with the print-out on the Ramsden report and I stayed to lend a hand. Did you have a good run up to town? Have you got yourselves drinks?' She spoke in a high, nervous voice and glanced at Harn in an uncertain manner, chatting on while she poured herself a drink. Gemma realised immediately that this was a different girl from the cool, self-contained Brenda that she had known before. The pressures of working in London, perhaps.

Harn didn't stay long. 'I'll leave you two girls to get yourselves sorted out,' he said. He turned to Brenda. 'Gemma says she wants to do some shopping. Have tomorrow morning off, both of you, and you can show her the best places.' He placed an envelope on the table in front of Gemma. 'A month's salary in advance,' he said. 'Plus the London increment. You'll need it, I imagine. I'll see you after lunch tomorrow.' He nodded to them both and left.

Brenda sank into a chair and kicked off her elegant, high-heeled black sandals. 'Whew! That's better, we can relax now. That man has a terrible effect on me. Makes me tense.' She didn't enlarge on that statement but sank back and closed her eyes.

Gemma waited in thoughtful silence. Was Brenda yet another of Harn's conquests? If so, it must have been some time in the past. She eyed a large silver-framed photograph next to the TV set. A man in Naval uniform with crinkly fair hair, laughing blue eyes and a firm faintly sensual mouth. Brenda's husband, no doubt. Married to a man as attractive as that there wouldn't be any room left in Brenda's life for Harn now, whatever there had been before. Or would there? Gemma wasn't sure. She had come into a new world where all the values were different from the ones she had grown up with.

If Brenda had been coming to live at *her* home, Beth would have been showing her her room, giving her a meal, making her feel wanted. As she sat looking at Brenda now, lying back with closed eyes taking no notice of her at all, Gemma suddenly felt lost and lonely.

'I usually drive in to the office,' Brenda said as she led Gemma into the underground car-park after lunch next day.' I have to have my car there because I never know when I'm going to be called out to some computer system that's playing up.' They reached the little white Mini and she unlocked the door. 'You'll want to be independent, so I'd advise a bus—I'll show you where you get it. Of course,' she added casually, 'if our times coincide I'll be happy to give you a lift.'

'Oh, I don't want to be a nuisance,' Gemma said hastily. 'You've been very kind to take me round the shops this morning, but I must get along under my own steam now.'

Brenda gave her a thoughtful look as they got into the car. 'Are you going to like working in London, do you think?'

'Oh yes, I'm sure I will, thank you,' Gemma said formally. She and Brenda had been curiously formal with each other since she arrived yesterday. When Brenda had been training her they had seemed to strike up a friendship, but here in London everything was different. Even this morning, as Brenda took her round the shops and advised her which clothes to buy, it hadn't really been very enjoyable. Brenda had seemed polite but rather bored and Gemma was glad when the shopping expedition came to an end.

Harn's office was in a high white, imposing building in the City. Brenda drove her car through a narrow tunnel and and into a parking space marked with her name, *Mrs B. Johnson,* painted in black letters on the cement. They went into the building by a back entrance and up in a lift to the tenth floor.

'We have this floor and the next one up,' she told Gemma, briskly leading the way into an open-plan office the size of two tennis courts. The whole area was divided by screens into a series of smaller units, each furnished with its own desks, electronic devices, computers, typewriters, telephones. Young men in business suits and careful hair-styles and girls who all looked to Gemma quite equal to being considered for the Secretary of the Year Award were sitting at the desks or moving about purposefully between them. Plate-glass windows lined one side of the office and feathery green plants in copper containers stood about in carefully chosen locations. The whole environment was light and cool and airy and about as different from the office of Durrants (Fine Paper) that Gemma had left behind in the Midlands as it could possibly be.

'It's so *quiet*,' she whispered to Brenda in amazement. 'All these people about, and hardly a sound!'

'Acoustic screens.' Brenda tossed the words carelessly over her shoulder, and Gemma felt like a new girl at school.

She was aware of some interested glances as she followed Brenda across the acres of cinnamon brown carpet. Brenda said 'Hullo,' and 'Hi,' to one or two of the people she passed. 'No use trying to introduce you to all these bods now,' she said, pushing open a glass door at the end of the office. 'We'll throw a party soon and you can meet them. They're quite a bright crowd.'

Up a short flight of stairs. 'Cloaks and loos here,' Brenda pointed the door out. Round a corner and up another few stairs to a corridor carpeted more thickly than the one below.

'Top Brass up here. That's Paul Jevon's office—he's Harn's second-in-command and quite a poppet. Next door's Mrs Fothergill—she's P.R. Very much on the ball—knows everybody in London. Then there's our accountant, Mr Weston—very keen. Next to him a reception and interview room.'

Gemma tried to take it all in, but butterflies were careering round her stomach at the thought that Harn was somewhere up here, behind one of these doors, and in a minute or two she would see him.

They had reached the end of the corridor now and Brenda opened a door and said, 'Hullo, Cynthia, I've brought your replacement along.'

Cynthia was a large, redhaired girl, and very pregnant. She pushed back her chair wearily and said, 'Thank heavens for that! The brat's getting so active that I can't concentrate.' She grimaced towards the inner door. 'Relations have got slightly strained this morning. I managed to jam the works——' she nodded towards a word-processor on her desk of the same kind that Gemma had been using '—and Durrant's been in a foul mood in consequence.'

She eyed Gemma up and down as she stood just inside the door in her neat navy-blue and white outfit—one of the ones she had bought this morning—with her fair hair tied back demurely and her mouth stretched in a smile that felt as if it were glued on. 'So you're the one that Durrant's bringing in from outside, are you?'

'Outside?' echoed Gemma.

'Outside our cosy little set-up here,' Cynthia explained. 'I hope you've been warned what to expect. Have you given her the low-down on our Miss Wright, Brenda?'

Brenda shook her head. 'I'll leave that to you.' There was a faint sound from behind and she said hastily, 'I must dash now, I've got an appointment at two.' She shot out of the office just as the door to the inner office opened and Harn appeared in the doorway. He looked very formidable standing there in a dark suit, his large body almost filling the space. Gemma felt her inside contract with something like fear.

'I'd like you to come in straight away, Gemma,' he said. He hardly looked at her and he sounded terse and distant. She tried to remind herself that this was business, and forget the commotion that was going on inside her as she remembered how yesterday he had held her in his arms and kissed her and called her a little witch.

'And you can get along home now, Cynthia,' he said. 'I'll put Gemma in the picture myself.' He added almost as an afterthought, 'Good luck for the big occasion—I hope he or she puts in an appearance without too much fuss. Keep in touch.' He disappeared into the inner sanctum.

Cynthia pulled a face behind his back as she began to open drawers and take out her belongings. 'Cut along, then,' she said to Gemma. 'For Pete's sake don't keep him waiting. And the best of British luck—you'll need it!'

Feeling very small, Gemma followed Harn into his office. When she got inside she felt even smaller. It was positively palatial and she had to walk across yards and yards of thick mole-coloured carpet to reach his enormous desk, situated in the far distance, where he was already seated.

She stood in front of the desk and waited while he frowned over some papers. Then he looked up and said irritably, 'Sit down, sit down.'

Gemma sat on the edge of the visitor's chair opposite.

He looked up at her at last, then glanced at the digital clock on his desk. 'I've a meeting at two, so there's no time to lose. Now, this is what I want you to get on with: There's a big Japanese contract in the pipeline and I need a report typing by tomorrow afternoon. It's all on tape ready for you and, as you'll see, that dimwit Cynthia has made a start. A deplorable start, I may say. See if you can sort it out and get it done by the time I get back later today. I can then revise it and you can print out the final copy tomorrow morning. O.K.?'

Gemma nodded. 'Yes, Mr Durrant,' she said crisply.

'You can use your own judgment as to the layout. I want the report on disc. You can use the word-processor? You've mastered it?' He shot the questions at her.

'Yes, Mr Durrant,' she said again. He wouldn't see her fingers crossed behind her back.

'Right, I'll go, then. My diary's here on my desk.' He tapped a red leather-covered book. 'No appointments at all for the next two days. You'd better put the phone on automatic reply—I don't want you to be interrupted while you're on this typing job. It must come first.' He crossed the office in three strides and the door swung behind him.

Gemma walked more slowly back to the secretary's office, and stared with something like horror at the mess of papers and notes on the desk. Cynthia had certainly made a start! 'In at the deep end,' she muttered. 'You're on your own now, chum.'

She sat down and switched on the word-processor and began to concentrate.

It was half-past five before Harn returned, but time had long since ceased to register for Gemma. Her eyes were aching with staring at the little white letters on the black screen; her hands were damp and her hair looked like a field of wheat when a rainstorm had flattened it. But the report was finished.

She didn't hear Harn coming towards her across the thick carpet because she was leaning back exhausted in the typing chair, her eyes closed, while the printer was at work, typing out the pages of the report. 'Well, how's it going?'

She jumped, catching her breath, and spun round in the swivel chair. 'I didn't hear you.'

'Too busy with the technology?' He sounded pleased with life now, in a much softer mood than the one he had gone out in. He leaned down and peered over her shoulder at the final page of the report appearing on the paper, while the printer clattered away frenziedly. 'Looks O.K.,' he said. 'Have much difficulty?'

'Well——' Gemma began cautiously, 'some of the terms were unfamiliar to me and I wasn't sure of the spelling. I tried to get hold of Brenda to ask her, but she was out and the person I spoke to in her department didn't help much.' That was an understatement. The woman behind the desk had looked daggers at her and snapped, 'I thought you were Mr Durrant's new secretary, surely you don't need to come down to us lower mortals asking for help.'

'Ha! That would be our Miss Wright. You may not find her very co-operative. She thought she should get the job when Cynthia departed. But I thought definitely otherwise.' He chuckled. 'I don't work very well with lemon-faced females!' He placed both hands on Gemma's shoulders. 'I like my secretaries to look decorative. Poor old Cynthia used to look quite pretty before she made the mistake of getting herself married and pregnant.' He chuckled again. 'Marriage—the great trap for males *and* females. Don't you go and get married, will you, Gemma?'

'I wasn't planning to just at present,' she said coldly.

'But I gather from your tone that you don't share my aversion to the married state?'

'Of course I don't,' she snapped. 'All girls—well, nearly all girls—want to get married.'

'And don't I know it!' he said mock-bitterly, just as the printer came to a stop with a 'peep'.

He pulled the paper out of the machine and picked up the little pile of pages on the desk. 'Now then,' he said, 'let's go over this together.'

It was after six by the time Harn had finished revising the report and the sheets of paper were covered with arrows and squiggles and underlinings. 'Think you can sort it all out tomorrow morning and have it printed out in time for my meeting at two?'

'I'm sure I can,' said Gemma, with more confidence than she felt. She would arrive very early, she planned, and give herself plenty of time. This was her first big assignment and she wasn't going to slip up on it if she could help it.

Harn stood up and stretched stiffly. 'All this sitting around doesn't suit me. I'll have to have a good work-out in the squash court in the morning.'

The phone rang. 'Who the hell's this at this hour?' Harn muttered as Gemma picked up the receiver.

'This is Mr Durrant's secretary speaking. Can I——'

A female voice cut through her polite announcement. 'I want to speak to Harn Durrant. Will you put me through to him straight away.'

Here we go again, Gemma thought. How do I get rid of this one? She said smoothly, 'I'm not sure if Mr Durrant has left or not. I'll go and see. Who shall I tell him, please?'

A husky laugh. 'Just say the Clicquot's on ice, waiting for him.'

Gemma put her hand over the receiver and looked up at Harn, her face expressionless. 'It seems there's some champagne waiting for you. Are you still here, or do you want me to go through the old routine again?'

He took the phone out of her hand. 'Yvonne? Yes—yes, I've been working on a job. Yes, I meant to ring you, but you know how it is.' He looked at his watch. 'Give me twenty minutes, I've got my car here. That champagne sounds very inviting.' The last sentence in a deliberately wolfish tone. ''Bye, darling.'

Gemma was tidying up her desk, trying hard not to listen, while every word went into her mind and stayed there, stinging like little poisoned arrows. Why on earth had she put the phone back on manual just before Harn came back? If she hadn't, the Yvonne female would have merely received a recorded message—and she could have yearned back a reply as throbbily as she liked, but Gemma would not have had to hear it.

Harn grinned at her as he replaced the receiver, a wicked glint in his dark eyes. 'I shan't need your help with this one, Gemma dear.'

She took her handbag from the top drawer and closed it carefully. 'May I go home now?'

'Certainly. Goodnight, Gemma. I'll lock up,' he said absently. He turned back to his own office without another glance in her direction.

'Goodnight, Mr Durrant,' she said, and then, because she must begin now this moment to be a new Gemma—a cool, modern girl who could give as good as she received—she added lightly, 'Enjoy your champagne.'

He turned his head and she saw his dark brows go up in surprise. For a moment they stared at each other. His face was expressionless, while her mouth curved in a quirky little smile, and only heaven knew how much it cost her. Then she went out of the office and closed the door behind her.

Blindly she made her way through the empty general office and down in the lift to the main lobby, where the night porter gave her a searching glance before he said, ''Night, miss.'

She mumbled a reply and almost ran past him and out into the street, where the cool air was blowing off the river and the crowds on the pavements were thinning out. She must stop thinking about Harn all the time, she told herself desperately as she joined the bus queue. She should have been prepared for the fact that he had a girl in London—and a girl he *didn't* want to get rid of. She pictured him walking into some plushy apartment and being enfolded in the white arms of a luscious girl in floating chiffon; throwing off his jacket and settling back into the corner of a deep sofa with velvet cushions, a champagne glass in one hand while the other arm held a softly yielding body against his.

The riddle was solved. The letter she had heard on the dictaphone was addressed to this Yvonne. She heard again his voice murmuring sexily, 'Love me? I adore you.' Damn, thought Gemma, blinking hot tears away. Oh, damn, damn, *damn!*

Beth had been right, Harn Durrant was a womaniser. From a personal point of view he wasn't worth her second thought. But it would be stupid to miss the chance of an interesting job just because she had got an adolescent crush on her boss. She would get over it in time, and this sickening grip of jealousy would loose its hold on her inside.

A bus pulled up and she climbed to the top deck. Looking down through the window, hazy with cigarette smoke, on to the slowly-moving pack of car roofs below, she repeated silently to herself, 'I'm a London girl now, a cool, modern girl, crisp and efficient, with an important, responsible job. I'm not soppy like Julia Moore, or brash and aggressive like Vera Knight. Or husky and seductive like this horrible Yvonne. I'm me, and I can hold out against this useless yearning I've got for Harn Durrant. I've jolly well got to!'

After which sensible pep-talk she took from her pocket the copy she had made of some of the more complicated functions of the word-processor, and concentrated on it (with one or two lapses) until she reached her stop.

CHAPTER SIX

'How about Friday for the party?' asked Brenda. 'It's time you got to know the general office bods. You've been in purdah in Harn's quarters since you arrived.'

Gemma giggled, 'You make it sound like a harem!' She tipped some cucumber wedges into a bowl of yoghurt. It was her turn to cook supper and she was making a chicken curry. Brenda was a super cook and could turn out exotic foreign dishes in double-quick time, but Gemma, whose cooking skills had been more prosaic up to now, was learning fast.

Brenda tucked away the work she had brought home with her and began to set the table in the small, well-equipped kitchen. 'That figures,' she said, and there was a faintly bitter edge to her voice. 'There's always been safety in numbers where Harn Durrant is concerned.'

'Don't I know it?' Gemma concentrated upon slicing chicken. 'My first job, back in Lessington, was to cope with his discarded girl-friends. So far,' she added casually, 'it hasn't been necessary here.'

There was a sudden silence, then Brenda clattered the cutlery on to the table. 'Just wait a bit until he gets tired of the glamorous Yvonne. She's been number one for some months now. It's about time for him to move on, I'd calculate.'

'Yvonne? Yes, she rang him up the other

evening.' Gemma was proud of her offhand manner; she could almost begin to believe that she had won her own private little battle. 'Who is she—do you know?'

'Actress. Mostly TV commercials—although I haven't seen her on the box lately. Maybe her luck's running out.' There was a spiteful note in Brenda's voice, but she didn't continue the conversation. 'What about the party? I think Friday would be a good day for most people.'

They spent most of the evening making plans, and when Gemma went to bed in the comfortable small bedroom overlooking the open area planted with trees and shrubs at the rear of the premises she reflected with satisfaction that she was really beginning to get settled down in London and adjust to the pace of the city.

The work was demanding, and she came home exhausted each evening, but she thought she was managing to satisfy Harn's demands on her. Their relationship had changed. He was very much the chief executive now, unapproachable except on business matters. The informality of Durrants (Fine Paper) office had stayed behind up in the Midlands. It was impossible to imagine herself telling him to shut up, as she remembered doing on one occasion.

Not that she saw very much of him; most of his time seemed to be taken up with meetings, either in his own office or elsewhere. This new deal that was in the pipeline with a Japanese firm was occupying all his time and energy, and he was pursuing it with a relentless determination that left Gemma gasping sometimes when she transcribed the notes and reports which, she guessed, he must have stayed up half the night working on. Most evenings she went home to leave him working, with the help of his personal computer, on abstruse problems of production and marketing. She wondered when he managed to relax. With Yvonne, no doubt. She could even contemplate that without the sickening turmoil in her stomach that she had felt the first time.

In short, she was pleased with her progress towards turning herself into a modern young woman in a top job, with Brenda always as her model. It wasn't much of an exaggeration when she wrote to Beth, who by now was having a deliriously happy time in Naples, 'Everything is going along splendidly and I'm learning fast and really enjoying life, Beth dear, so don't worry about me.'

The day of the party turned out specially busy and Gemma began to get edgy when the clock had come round to six-thirty and Harn was still showing no sign of releasing her.

She was in Harn's office, taking instructions about information she was in progress of obtaining in connection with the Japanese deal, when suddenly he stopped speaking and said curtly, 'What's the matter with you tonight, Gemma? You're as jumpy as blazes. Got a date or something?'

The perfect secretary doesn't fuss when she happens to be kept late. 'N-no,' she stammered, 'I'm all right.'

He regarded her keenly. 'As I once remarked before, you're a rotten liar. Come on, let's have it.'

She grinned wryly. 'It's just that Brenda is giving a small party tonight and I wanted to be in time to help her with the preparations. But it doesn't matter a bit. Please let's go on.' She poised her pencil over her notebook and waited.

He pushed the papers aside. 'There's no immediate hurry for this. We'll leave it till the morning.' He sat back and studied her face. 'How's it going, Gemma? Are you settling down and enjoying London?'

'Oh yes, thank you, Mr Durrant,' she said sedately. 'Brenda has made me very comfortable.'

'And provided you with some prospective boy-friends, no doubt?'

'Well, no, there hasn't been much time for socialising yet. This party is mostly for me to meet the rest of the staff here.'

'I see.' He went on looking at her for what seemed a very long time in silence until she began to feel embarrassed under his scrutiny. Then he blinked as if he were remembering something and said quickly, 'Right, Gemma, you get away now and cut your sandwiches. Enjoy your party,' he added casually, turning back to his papers.

'Thank you, Mr Durrant,' Gemma was on her feet in a flash. 'Goodnight.'

'Goodnight,' he said absently, and she knew he had already forgotten her.

By half-past nine people began drifting in. Brenda evidently considered it the normal time, although it seemed to Gemma very late to begin a party. But at least it had given her time to shower, and do her hair and make-up, and dress in the cornflower-blue crêpe with the finely-pleated skirt and silver belt, which was the only dress she had that was suitable for a party. She hadn't yet bought any party clothes in London; she was waiting to see how the money worked out before she splashed out on luxuries. But this dress was nearly new, and the only time she had worn it—at a friend's wedding—everyone said it suited her.

The big living room of the flat had been transformed. The chairs were pushed back to leave plenty of room for the guests to mingle. The glass-topped table was loaded with mouthwatering snacks and dishes of nuts and crisps and savoury biscuits and the fridge was stacked with bottles of wine. The lights were shaded, throwing a pink glow over the whole room, and a hi-fi moaned softly in one corner.

Brenda looked gorgeous in a grass-green satin sheath, slit at the sides, her raven hair shining like black satin. She was more animated than Gemma had seen her yet, flitting about, greeting the guests at the door with hugs and cries as if they were long-lost friends instead of colleagues with whom she had spent most of the day working. Gemma hardly recognised any of them in their party get-ups. Her own experience of parties up to now was of the student variety, but this one was very different. Not a pair of jeans in sight or a scruffy hair-do. Undoubtedly, these young people had been hand-picked by Harn Durrant, and they were bound for success in the business world.

Gemma began to understand why parties began late; the girls' make-up wasn't the kind that could be slapped on in minutes, and their hair-dos had the kind of casual elegance that takes hours to produce. Every one of them looked as if they might have been modelling for one of the glossy magazines. Their clothes were probably off the peg, but they wore them with confidence and flair. The men were carefully groomed too, even a trifle exotic, and smelling rather too much of aftershave, Gemma considered, and she didn't really like men in earrings.

At first Brenda introduced Gemma casually to each newcomer, but soon the room was full of chatter and laughter and it was almost impossible to catch anybody's name. She stood by the wall looking around and trying to memorise them all. The only person she had spoken to previously in the office, except for saying 'hullo' in the lift, was Miss Wright, who worked in Brenda's department and who had been decidedly testy on that first day. She picked her out quite easily now, on the far side of the room, talking to another woman, their heads close together, the two of them looking out of place among the trendy young people around them. Miss Wright was an extremely plain woman of thirty-odd, with lanky nondescript hair and an unfortunate figure. She had chosen to wear bright yellow, and Gemma smothered a giggle as she remembered that Harn had called her a lemon-faced female.

A plump man with a round, red face and a droopy moustache put a glass of wine in Gemma's hand and said, 'You're up on the top floor, aren't you? Harn's new acquisition? Lucky devil, *he* is!' He leered at her out of hazy, hot brown eyes. He had quite certainly been drinking a fair amount before he arrived. He slid an arm round her waist. 'I'm Vincent Bartholomew,' he pronounced the syllables carefully. 'On the road.'

Gemma moved a little to detach herself. 'On the road?' she murmured.

'A rep, darling. I sell the hardware.' His arm returned more purposefully.

'Oh, yes?' she said vaguely. 'How nice for you. Will you excuse me, I think some more bottles are needed from the fridge.' She made a beeline for the kitchen.

Brenda was washing glasses. 'I should have hired more, we've got a fair number of gatecrashers. You mingling all right, Gemma? Getting to know everybody?'

'Oh yes, thank you,' fibbed Gemma tactfully. 'I think it's going very well, don't you?'

Brenda gave her a sideways glance and said, 'Sorry I had to invite May Wright and her pal from Accounts. They don't exactly add to the fun and games, but May works with me, and I couldn't very well leave her out. Have you encountered her in the office yet?'

Gemma arranged glasses on a tray. 'I went down looking for you, the first day I was here. I got stuck on some of the terms I hadn't met before. Miss Wright wasn't exactly helpful, and that's an understatement.'

Brenda smiled tightly. 'Oh, you don't want to take any notice of her. Everyone knows what she's like. Would you take these glasses in, Gemma? The drink's going to run out soon unless someone brings some more bottles.'

Gemma loaded her tray and, balancing it carefully, pushed open the kitchen door with her foot. Here she stopped as she caught a glimpse of a yellow dress, just on the other side of the door. Miss Wright's voice had a curiously carrying quality, and, although she was talking confidentially to someone on her other side, every word carried clearly to Gemma who stood, holding her tray against her hip, frozen to the spot.

'——and he's brought back this chit of a girl he picked up in the Midlands. And you know what *that* means, don't you, dear?' A significant pause. 'He calls her his secretary, but she doesn't know the first thing about the business. She's been down to me already, begging for help.' A thin snigger. 'After what happened with you-know-who, you'd think he'd have the decency to keep his floozies away from the office, wouldn't you? I call it disgusting!'

There was a murmur from her other side, which Gemma didn't catch, and then the unpleasant nasal voice again. 'Come on, dear, let's go. I know how this party will be later on, and I destest that kind of thing. I only came because it would have looked odd if I'd refused.' The voice dropped to a whisper. 'After all, I have to work with B.J., unfortunately.'

Gemma waited until they had moved away before she went out into the living room. She felt horribly uncomfortable. Overheard conversations should be forgotten as soon as possible, she considered, and she hadn't really been very surprised at what she had heard May Wright say about herself. It was just what an envious, petty woman would say. But that bit about 'you-know-who' and 'B.J.'—who could only be Brenda—stuck in her mind as she circulated, filling glasses, and playing the hostess. Forget it, she told herself, it's no business of yours.

Dancing had started now to a disco tune and Gemma didn't lack for partners. The men were queueing up to dance with her, and in the inevitable exchange of banter she managed to hold her own and began to feel that this was fun and that she was one of them, and was enjoying herself.

Gradually the food ran out and most of the wine. Then a big man with side-whiskers and tight purple velvet trousers turned up carrying more bottles, and the drink began to circulate again.

The atmosphere got hot and sultry. The lights were dimmed down to almost nothing and the music changed to a smoochy beat. Couples swayed together, locked in each other's arms. Gemma saw Vincent Bartholomew approaching, and escaped into her bedroom. Giggles and squeals came from the direction of the bed and she retreated again. The Bartholomew man was waiting on the other side of the door and grabbed her as she emerged.

'Been lookin' for you, darlin'.' His voice was slurred and the hand that groped for her waist was hot and damp. 'C'm and dance.'

Gemma looked round desperately for Brenda, but she was over on the other side of the room near the door, sitting on the floor, her head on the shoulder of a fair man who looked like a rugger player. There was no one else Gemma could appeal to and no escape without being rude. She wished she had the confidence to be rude, but this was Brenda's party and she couldn't make an unpleasant scene.

The next few minutes were horrible. The Bartholomew man was being utterly insufferable. 'Don't *do* that!' she hissed, trying to drag herself away.

'Aw, c'm on, sweetie, be a sport!' His breath was hot and unpleasant, near her face.

'Let me *go*!' She began to struggle helplessly. Nobody else seemed to be taking the slightest bit of notice.

Suddenly, from nowhere, a hand came between her and the Bartholomew man and separated them. A voice, curt and furious, said, 'You heard what the lady said, now get the hell out of here.'

Gemma saw Vincent Bartholomew's full-moon face, crimson and foolish, fading into the background. Her arm was held firmly. 'Let's go,' said Harn Durrant. 'I'm sure you've had enough of this.'

He propelled her through the crush of swaying couples to the door. Gemma heard him call out above the throb of the hi-fi, 'I'm borrowing my secretary for a short time, Brenda. Urgent work,' and then they were down the stairs and out into the blessed cool of the night air.

'Want to walk to my car?' Harn said briskly. 'It's just around the corner. Or will you hang on here while I get it?' He bent down and studied her face in the light from the entrance. 'You're not drunk, are you?'

'Certainly not!' Gemma said indignantly.

He laughed. 'Don't sound so outraged! I know how Brenda's parties tick, and you're too young to be launched into that sort of thing, my child. Which is why I came to rescue you, and not without reason, it seems. That drip Batholomew was on the prowl, wasn't he?'

They started to walk along the dark, nearly-empty streets, and he linked his arm loosely with hers. Gemma was aware of a stirring of excitement at his touch, which she subdued with an effort, thinking how odd it was that the touch of one man

could fill one with loathing while the touch of
another man sent you swinging on a star.

'We'll go to my flat,' said Harn as they found
his car and got into it. 'You can stay long enough
to make it look as if we'd been working and then
I'll take you back to the party.'

'Make it *look* as if we'd been working?' Gemma
queried, puzzled.

'Certainly, that's the idea.'

'Then—then that isn't why you came for me? I
thought it might be something to do with a late
phone call to Japan?'

He shook his head. 'Not tonight.'

Gemma stole a glance at the strong, chiselled
profile as his hand went out to the self-starter.
'Then——' she swallowed '——why are you
taking all this trouble on my account?' She was
beginning to feel very uneasy.

'I ask myself that same question.' The engine
purred into life. 'Let's say you're very young and I
feel a certain responsibility towards you. You once
asked me if I ever considered anyone besides
myself—well, here's your answer, and I must say it
surprises me as much as it no doubt surprises you.'
With which cryptic reply he put the car into gear
and it moved smoothly off.

All the way to wherever it was Harn was taking
her Gemma was beset with a variety of emotions,
changing from near-panic to utter bliss. She tried
to remember how many glasses of wine she had
drunk at the party, but already the party was
becoming a vague memory. The reality was that
she was sitting beside Harn in his luxurious car, in
the early hours of the morning, swooping along
the darkened London streets. It was heaven, it was

temptation, and she felt more confused and disturbed with every passing moment.

This was London, she reminded herself, this was the Big Time. This was what she had wanted, and it was the most exciting thing she had ever done in her life. But she was frightened too, because she didn't know what lay at the end of the drive, when they reached Harn's flat. *Does* a man like she knew Harn Durrant to be take a girl to his flat at this hour and expect nothing more of her than a little polite conversation? There seemed only one answer to that, and she didn't know what she was going to do about it. But she felt a hazy recklessness stirring inside her, and she snuggled up to him, conscious of the warmth of his lean, hard-muscled body and the healthy male smell of the man.

He glanced down and she could feel him smiling although she couldn't see his face. 'Tired?' he asked softly.

'Um,' she murmured. 'It's way past my bedtime.'

He laughed aloud. 'We'll have to see what we can do about that,' he said.

Gemma sat up straight, pulling herself away from him with an effort. 'You're not thinking of——' she began, because if he was she wanted to know in advance.

'Putting you to bed and singing a lullaby? The thought had occurred to me. But there's only one lullaby I know to sing to a pretty girl in bed, and you might be too young to recognise the tune.'

He was fooling, of course. If he really meant to get her into his bed he wouldn't be making a joke of it. But he had this talent for turning the conversation into channels that all led in the same direction, and Gemma sat still and said nothing more until the car drew up outside a tall house in a square. Before Harn switched off the car lights they fell on the leaves of the trees, turning them to silver. It was very quiet in this backwater of London—only the ceaseless faint rumble of traffic in the distance. The night was still and warm and in the glimmer of the streets lights the houses looked imposing, with porticos and railings and steps leading up to heavy front doors.

'Come along in,' said Harn. 'We'll make ourselves coffee and you can tell me the story of your life.

She giggled. Yes, she must have drunk too much wine; that was why she felt so light and floaty as they climbed the steps arm in arm. Inside, the lobby was plushy and luxurious with soft concealed lighting and velvety carpet. They walked up to the first floor and Harn put his key into the lock of a white front door with his name on it and ushered her in, turning on the light as he went.

He stood in the middle of a small, square hall. 'Lounge, kitchen, bathroom, bedroom,' he announced, indicating each door in turn. 'Take your pick.'

She moved towards the bathroom. 'I'd like a wash,' she said, carefully avoiding looking at the bedroom door.

'Right, I'll go and put the coffee on.'

'I suppose we couldn't——' Gemma began. 'No, it doesn't matter.'

'Of course it matters,' he said, suddenly sounding eager. 'Couldn't what?'

'I was going to say I suppose we couldn't have

tea instead of coffee,' Gemma said, and he burst into a roar of laughter.

'Funny child, of course we could,' he said. And then, 'I tend to forget how very young you are.'

She pushed open the bathroom door and went inside. What had her age to do with whether they had tea or coffee? she wondered, and then dismissed the question as unanswerable.

It was a man's bathroom, all brown and tortoiseshell. Gemma opened the cupboard doors but couldn't see any trace of Yvonne. No French perfume, or skin lotions. No flimsy robe hanging behind the door. No lipstick on the towels. But of course, he wouldn't bring Yvonne here, no doubt she had a silken love-nest of her own somewhere, Gemma thought gloomily. Then she cheered up. Wherever it was, Harn wasn't with her in it tonight. He had worried about her—Gemma— however unlikely it seemed, and had come out specially to make sure she was all right, and that was marvellous.

She swilled her hot cheeks and dried them on a fleecy golden-yellow towel that smelled of Harn's aftershave. There was a bottle of it on a glass shelf and she took off the stopper and had a good sniff, which gave her shivers down her back. Indeed, she would have to be careful, if she didn't want to end up as just one more on Harn's long list of discarded girl-friends. She just wished she hadn't drunk so much wine.

She went out into the kitchen where Harn was lolling against a work-top, waiting for the kettle to boil. He looked wonderful, she thought, in black pants and a pink shirt that would make any other man look washed-out. There was nothing washed-out about this man, he was fabulous, and her heart gave a small leap and began to beat very quickly as he smiled at her, the curving dark lashes lifting at the corners.

'Better?' he queried.

'I'm fine now—the party got rather sticky.'

'Ah!' he said. The kettle boiled and he poured water into a white china pot with green dragons on it. 'Not your kind of party?'

'Not really,' she admitted. 'I wasn't enjoying it much. It was rather too—what's the word?—rather too anonymous, if you know what I mean.'

He carried the tray into the lounge and put it on a low table beside a deep, buttoned velvet sofa, into which he sank, patting the place beside him.

'Yes, I think I know what you mean. You're choosy about who you allow to take liberties.' His mouth quirked as he added, 'And very right and proper, too.'

Gemma seated herself at the other end of the sofa. 'All right, so I'm a small town girl,' she said, with as much dignity as she could muster, 'and no doubt I'm naïve and unsophisticated and I seem silly to you, but—yes, that's exactly how I feel about it.'

Harn poured tea and pushed a cup along the table towards her. Then he leaned back in the corner of the sofa, crossing his long legs and resting one arm along the back, and studied her face in silence for so long that her mouth went dry and she had to take a long gulp of tea.

At last he asked, 'What do you want out of life, Gemma? What did you hope to get out of coming to London?'

'Experience,' she said promptly.

'And you hoped I would provide that experience for you?'

'Yes, I did,' she said seriously. 'I thought if I could make the grade as your secretary, if only for a short time, and train in the modern technology, then I should be in a good position to apply for any job, and not have to start at the bottom, as I should have done in the ordinary course. I want to be able to pay my way at home and help my sister, who's done so much for me all my life.'

'Um.' He shook his head slowly. 'And was that the only kind of experience you hoped I'd provide?'

Her eyes widened and she could feel the warmth rising to her cheeks, and was thankful for the soft, concealed lighting. 'Y-yes, of course,' she stammered. Then, gaining courage, and because she had to make this quite clear to him, just in case— she added, 'If you're thinking that I had ambitions to become one in your long line of discarded girl-friends please forget it. The prospect doesn't appeal.'

He turned his devilish look on her and the thick dark lashes swept his cheeks. 'Couldn't I persuade you if I really tried? If you want to be a London girl you'll have to learn the ways of the big bad city, you know, and I doubt if there are many virgins around of—what's your age?—nearly nineteen, isn't it?'

He was making a joke of it, and that was a kind of relief. She laughed back and a dimple appeared in her right cheek. 'Then I'll just have to be in the minority, won't I?'

He poured himself a second cup of tea. 'If you change your mind may I have the first refusal?'

'Certainly, Mr Durrant,' she said gravely, and passed her cup to be refilled.

As he passed it back their hands touched and she snatched her hand away, appalled at the sudden turmoil inside her.

He put the cup down carefully and sat back in his corner, his eyes never leaving her face. There was a long silence while their eyes met and Gemma tried to look away but was totally unable to. At last, when the silence had become almost unbearable, Harn leaned forward and covered her hand with his. His fingers were dry and smooth and strong. 'Don't let's pretend it's not there, Gemma. It started way back in the office in Lessington. We seem to do something to each other, don't we? You want me as much as I want you, admit it.'

Here it was, then—what she had dreaded and yet longed for, and she wasn't ready to make a choice. Not here, in this softly-lit apartment, with his fingers touching hers and promising so much more by their pressure.

She drew a quivering breath. 'No, it's too soon and it's not right. I work for you, and don't they say you shouldn't mix business with pleasure—'

'They say a lot of silly things,' he said, and moved towards her, his arm resting along the back of the sofa behind her, his other hand still clasping hers. He gave her time to move away, but she couldn't move an inch. Every nerve ending on her skin prickled with awareness; her whole body was alive and expectant. It was like nothing she had ever felt before, and it was fear and wonder.

His arm lowered and enclosed her and he drew her towards him. 'It's no good fighting it, my little

Gemma, it will get you in the end, you know, and you don't want to make a start with someone like Vincent Thingummy, do you?'

No word of love—just pure, unashamed sex. Suddenly she could hear his voice again as she had heard it on the tape—'Love me? I adore you.' *That* had been love, but he wasn't saying that to her. He wasn't even pretending to be in love with her. It's all wrong, she thought wildly as his head lowered and another, stronger thought surfaced: Oh no, what am I going to do? If he kisses me, I'm lost.

His mouth came down on hers, his lips brushing hers rhythmically, then closing over her mouth, easing her lips apart, taking his time, while wave after wave of ecstasy coiled through her. Why not—why not? she thought, weak with longing. It has to happen some time, as he said.

His hand slipped into the deep vee of her neckline and closed over the soft swell of her breast, while his other hand moved down and stroked her thigh. She heard his breathing quicken and felt a kind of elation, almost power. And then sanity left her completely and her hands went convulsively round his waist, pressing his body against hers, kissing him with an abandon that shocked her even while she gloried in it. He pulled her dress off her shoulders and his mouth moved over her neck and down to find the hollow between her breasts.

'God, you're lovely—so lovely——' he groaned, and his movements became more urgent. She could feel his heart thudding against her and her own heart pounding in response. He pulled down the zipp at the back of her dress and his fingers fumbled with the fastening of her bra, loosening it at last. In the soft light her skin glimmered whitely as he ripped off his own shirt and then she felt his weight on her, flesh against flesh, and heard her own moan of abandonment.

That was when the telephone began to sound on the other side of the room. 'Let it ring, blast it,' Harn muttered, and went on kissing her, but something had changed; there was a suddenly lowering of tension as if a stretched spring had been pulled to the utmost and then released and collapsed against itself.

The ringing went on and on, more intrusive because it was a soft purr and not a shrill bell. The noise seemed to fill Gemma's head like cotton wool and she twisted her body away with a convulsive shudder. 'Answer it,' she muttered.

Harn dragged himself up and crossed the room. 'Yes? What? Yes, she is.' His eyes never left Gemma as he spoke. She swung her legs round and pulled her dress over her shoulders, struggling with the back zip. And then, curtly, 'All right, all right, I'll tell her.' He slammed the receiver back on to its cradle.

He came back and stood staring down at her, his dark eyes unreadable. 'That was Brenda. Do you want to go back to the party? It seems most of them are leaving.'

Gemma was suddenly overcome by guilt. Brenda had arranged the party for her and she had just walked out. It was unforgivable. 'Yes,' she said miserably, 'I should never have come away.'

'Perhaps you're right,' Harn said grimly. Seeing her still struggling with the zip, he leaned over and fixed it matter-of-factly. 'Saved by the bell,' he said dryly. 'Or rather, by Brenda's suspicious mind.'

He fastened up his shirt and pushed his dark, tousled hair back. 'You won't believe this, Gemma, but when I brought you here I truly didn't mean any of this——' he gestured towards the sofa '—to happen. I guess my self-control isn't as strong as I imagined. Now, go along and brush your hair and tidy yourself up and I'll drive you back.'

The drive was accomplished in complete silence. When the car drew up Harn got out and opened the door for Gemma without offering his hand. In the shadows his face looked shuttered. She hesitated. What could she say? I'm glad the great seduction didn't happen? Had he been telling the truth when he said he hadn't meant it to happen?

'Goodnight,' she muttered, and dived into the entrance and stumbled up the stairs.

The guests had all gone. The living room was empty except for Brenda, who sat alone amid the residue of the party—dirty glasses and dishes, cigarette ends spilling out of ashtrays and trampled into the carpet, the stale smell of smoke hanging over everything.

Gemma walked over to her. 'Brenda, I really am sorry—please forgive me for leaving. Harn wanted me for some work, you see, and——' The words died in her throat as she saw Brenda's face, white and haggard, two scarlet spots on her cheekbones.

'Work? Don't give me that, you little tart! I thought you were a decent girl, not a common tramp!'

Gemma recoiled with shock. Then, impulsively, she went forward and put a hand on the other girl's arm. 'Brenda, you've got it wrong. I didn't—

I *had* to go with him when he came for me. You know he puts calls through to Japan in the middle of the night. The time-change——'

Her hand was flung off violently. 'Oh, shut up, you make me sick! You went to his flat, and what did you expect to do when you got there?' Brenda laughed stridently. 'You forget I've known Harn Durrant for quite a time. I know what happens when he has a girl in his flat in the middle of the night, and it's nothing to do with phone calls to Japan. Oh yes, I know what's been going on, I can picture it all very well!'

Her face changed, became ugly and twisted, and Gemma cowered back against the door as horrible gutter words came shooting towards her. This couldn't be Brenda Johnson—the cool, collected modern young woman whom Gemma had hoped one day to be like. This was a woman eaten up and made mad by jealousy and hate.

'Get out—get out——!' Brenda screamed at last, losing all control. 'I won't have you here, coming straight from his bed! I won't put up with your filthy——' The obscene words came pouring out and Gemma covered her ears with her hands. The white, contorted face with the red blotches came nearer and nearer, getting larger and larger as it came. It was like some terrifying nightmare. Frenziedly Gemma groped behind her for the catch of the door, turned it, and then she was stumbling down the stairs as if all the furies were pursuing her.

Outside in the cool night air, she leaned against the wall, gasping for breath, shaking with fright. It had all been so sudden, so utterly unexpected. Childishly she screwed her hands into fists and thrust them against her eyes as if she could blot out the ugly scene.

After a while she began to feel more calm. All was quiet and dark and the coolness that had been so welcome a minute ago turned to a cold that made her shiver. The blue crêpe dress gave her no protection and she had not stopped to put on a coat when Harn came to the party to collect her.

She peered at her wrist-watch and saw that it was ten past three. Where could she go at this time of night, with no luggage and only small change in the handbag which she found she was still gripping as if it were a dangerous snake? She looked around. That way the streets led to the City; the other way to the river.

She was shivering with cold and shock and misery. Was this the end of her great adventure, of all her hopes of life in London? She thought it was. Tomorrow—if tomorrow ever came—she would get on a train and go home. She thought longingly of the little house in Lessington. Even if Beth wasn't there it would be familiar and warm and comforting. But somehow she had to get through the rest of the night.

She began to walk towards the City. Not the river. The river brought ghoulish thoughts of muggings, and men sleeping rough, and her imagination began to work overtime. She walked the length of the apartment building and turned the corner. Then she let out a strangled scream and her body went rigid as the shadow of a man descended on her.

She turned and began to run, stumbling over the uneven surface of the roadway. Her satin pumps caught in a rough patch and she fell to the ground, whimpering with pain and terror.

He was upon her now, his great hands closing round her, pulling her to her feet. She began to fight feebly, threshing out with her fists and her handbag went flying.

'Stop it, you stupid child! It's me—Harn.'

She blinked up and saw that it was. 'Thank God—thank God——' she babbled, clutching his arm to hold herself up. 'I thought——'

His face began to swim in the gloom. Round and round it went until it blanked out entirely.

Gemma had fainted.

When she came to herself Gemma was sitting in Harn's car and he was leaning over her, stroking her hair back from her face, murmuring something she couldn't hear.

She stuggled to sit up, her teeth chattering. Harn's arm around her was infinitely comforting. 'You all right, Gemma? Phew, you had me worried!'

She licked her dry lips. 'I—I'm sorry. I don't know what happened——'

'You passed out at my feet.'

Memory returned and she cringed inside. 'Oh lord, yes—I was terrified! I thought you were one of those muggers you read about.'

He laughed ruefully. 'I've been called a good many things, but never before a mugger.'

'Oh, I didn't—I mean——' She began to weep helplessly.

His arm tightened around her. 'It's all right, baby, it's all right, I was only joking. Now, you lie back and relax and we'll get going. I take it you'd rather not go back to Brenda's flat?'

Horrified at the idea, she blurted out wildly, 'No—no—I can't go back there. I *can't*!'

He laid her gently in the corner of the seat and patted her hand. 'Then you shan't,' he said firmly. 'I should never have suggested you going there in the first place. I can see I've been a bloody fool on many counts where you're concerned, Gemma. Never mind, it's not too late to put things right.'

She didn't know what he was talking about, but it didn't seem to matter. She lay back and closed her eyes while he started the car, and almost immediately the soft hum of the powerful engine soothed her and she dropped into an uneasy sleep.

His voice wakened her. 'We're here. I'm afraid it's the same old spot, but there's nowhere else I can think of to take you.'

He half lifted her out of the car and supported her up the stairs to his flat. 'This time there's no argument,' he smiled. 'You're really going straight into my bed, with a hot-water bottle, if I can find where my Mrs Mopp has hidden it.' He lowered her on to the bed and took a fleecy camel-coloured robe out of the closet and wrapped it round her. 'There you are, Gemma—now you look like a teddy bear.'

She smiled back wanly. She might have been six years old, the way he was treating her. But the surprising thing was that he could be kind—and gentle—and—and *nice*. She wouldn't have believed it possible. She lay back and let the comfort and warmth seep into her and pushed away those awful moments outside Brenda's flat, when she felt so terribly alone.

Harn was back in a few minutes with a hot water bottle and a tray. 'More tea,' he said cheerfully. 'Good and strong and sweet. You've had a shock, my child. Want to tell me about it?'

She pulled herself up and cuddled the hot water bottle under the camel robe and sipped the hot tea. 'Nothing to tell, really. Brenda was a bit—difficult, that's all, and I thought it better to get out of the way.'

He sat down on the edge of the bed. 'Which charitable account, when translated, reads that Brenda threw one of her tantrums and scared the wits out of you and you escaped without even waiting to find a coat. A good thing I hung about to make sure you were O.K. I had a sort of idea that something like this might happen.' As she would have spoken he lifted a hand and went on, 'No, Gemma, no good trying to evade the issue. Brenda Johnson is an excellent employee, but unfortunately she can get very hysterical at times. The main trouble is that she shouldn't be married to a sailor who's away from home for long periods.' He glanced at her under the thick, dark lashes and added, 'If you know what I mean.'

'I think so,' Gemma murmured. 'She needs a man.'

'Precisely,' he said crisply. 'Unfortunately she has at various times tried to pick on me to oblige—without any success, I may add. I steer very clear of married women, they're apt to cause too many complications.'

'I see,' Gemma said slowly. 'That explains it, then.' It didn't really explain it—not Brenda's violent attack, her frenzied accusations.

'I'm sorry to have let you in for this,' he went on. 'It was something I didn't consider. I'm afraid I took it for granted that Brenda had come to terms with things, after a very rocky patch, and I thought it would be good for her—and for you—

to get to know each other and provide company. But I see I was wrong. Of course, we'll have to find some other accommodation for you. Meanwhile, have a good sleep for what's left of the night, and we'll sort things out in the morning. You're very welcome to my bed—I'll be quite comfy on the sofa in the next room.' He opened the door of a closet and yanked out an armful of blankets. 'Sleep well, little one.' He bent and kissed her forehead. 'And don't worry. Everything will come right, you'll see.'

When he had gone Gemma lay back in the bed and closed her eyes, and great tears formed behind her lids and slid down her cheeks. It was no good kidding herself any longer about adolescent crushes. What she felt for Harn Durrant was a long way from that. She was deep in love as a woman is in love; so deep that it terrified her because it was inconceivable that he should ever be in love with her. He wasn't a man who would find it necessary to talk of love—he had proved that earlier this evening.

And yet—and yet—there *was* a woman he loved, or had loved. She kept hearing his voice saying, 'Love me? I adore you.' Would she ever find out who that letter had been addressed to?

Forget it, Gemma, she told herself. You'll never hear him say those words to you.

There was warmth all round her, but she began to shiver. She drew the camel gown closer and pulled the duvet up over her chin and snuggled down in Harn's bed.

This, she thought with black humour that cut through her like a knife, was the first and last time she would ever sleep in it.

CHAPTER SEVEN

GEMMA was dragged out of a long sleep by the sound of the telephone peep-peeping beside the bed. She stretched out and fumbled the receiver off the hook, blinking round the unfamiliar room as the memory of last night became clearer by the moment. Of course—she was in Harn's flat—in Harn's bed.

'Hullo?' she yawned, swinging her legs out of bed with an effort. It would be a call for Harn, of course. The trained secretary in her added automatically, 'This is Mr Harn Durrant's flat.' Where was Harn, and what time was it?

'Oh, is it indeed?' said a female voice from the other end of the line. 'And who might you be?' The tone was distinctly nasty.

There wasn't any time to think. 'I'm Gemma Lawson, Mr Durrant's secretary.'

'Really?' The tone became even nastier. 'And do you usually start work at Mr Durrant's flat at this hour of the morning?'

Gemma stared round and saw a red leather travelling clock on the bedside table. It was eight forty-five. 'I—I——' she began. How could she begin to explain to a stranger? 'Shall I get Mr Durrant for you?' she floundered helplessly.

A scathing laugh. 'Isn't he lying there beside you? No, thanks, it'll do later.' There was a loud click as the receiver was slammed down at the other end.

Gemma shrugged and got out of bed. Another of Harn's girl-friends, of course. Even here she couldn't get away from them—more than ever here, she thought bitterly. She was almost sure she had recognised the voice and that it was Yvonne, the one who had promised him champagne on ice the other evening. Oh well——

Dispiritedly she tightened the girdle of the camel robe that she had spent the night in and went in search of Harn.

It didn't take long to discover that he wasn't in the flat. A note was propped against the kettle in the kitchen, and Gemma unfolded it while she boiled water for tea.

'Gemma——' she read, written in Harn's spiky black writing, familiar to her by now, 'I've gone to Brenda's to get you some clothes. Back soon. H.'

The kettle boiled and she made tea and carried it into the bedroom. When she had drunk it she felt slightly better. It seemed to her that her life was in a horrible muddle at present, but there was no time to sit down and think things out calmly— even if she had been capable of doing it—so she would just have to live an hour at a time and see what happened.

After a shower in Harn's tortoiseshell bathroom she felt refreshed and more ready to face the day. She wrapped a green bath-towel round her and padded back into the bedroom. To her horror Harn stood leaning against the doorpost, a wide grin on his face.

'Very pretty!' he mused, his glance resting on the smooth skin of her arms and neck and the delightful shape of her legs that showed beneath the towel.

'Oh!' gasped Gemma, and turned to run back to the bathroom, but caught her foot in the hem of the towel, which slipped down and fell in a fleecy bundle on to the carpet. Harn stooped and picked it up before she could move and draped it carefully round her pink body, fresh and moist from her shower. For a moment his arms closed round her and hugged her tightly. 'Lovely Gemma,' he sighed. 'What a pity we haven't an hour to spare, but duty calls. There's this meeting with Mr Okimo at twelve.'

Gemma managed to pull her wits together, at least partially. She grabbed the towel tightly round her and said, 'Oh lord, yes, I wanted to get in early to print out the report for you. It's all there on disc and you revised it yesterday.'

He nodded. 'I'll get the Wright woman to get on with printing it out until you get in. She's quite capable of doing that if I find the disc for her.'

Gemma bit her lip. 'Couldn't it wait until I come? I'd be very——'

Harn shook his head. 'I want it done straight away, I need to go through it again before I leave. This is the crunch meeting, you know. No, you have some breakfast and take your time. You'd better ring for a taxi when you're ready—I don't suppose you'd find your way from here and I won't stop to direct you now. I've brought you some clothes——' he nodded towards her travelling bag on the bed—— 'and there's a letter that came for you this morning. By the way, Brenda's very chastened about what happened last night. I think she wants to make it up with you, but I still feel you shouldn't go back there. Anyway, we'll sort it all out later, I must dash now.'

He didn't exactly dash. He lingered for another long appreciative look at Gemma's slender body wrapped in the green towel, and then, with one of his devilish grins, he turned and went out of the flat.

Gemma stood where he had left her, thinking about nothing much, but feeling a good deal. Her mind was far away, floating on a cloud somewhere, when the key sounded in the front door. He had come back! She clutched the towel more firmly round her and turned to the open bedroom door, her heart racing.

Then it plummeted downwards, for it was not Harn who came across the hall and straight into the bedroom, but a staggeringly beautiful girl in a white fur jacket and a scarlet culotte skirt. Her hair was ash-blonde, her skin was perfection and the eyes that regarded Gemma with contempt were clear sea-green.

She stood with one hand on the door-knob in the effortlessly elegant pose of a model. 'So— you're the new secretary I've heard about, are you?' The perfect mouth curled into a sneer. 'It hasn't taken you long to get into Harn's bed.'

Gemma tried desperately to keep her cool, but being naked except for a bath-towel put her at a distinct disadvantage. 'Look, Miss—er——' she began, 'you've got it all wrong. I hadn't anywhere to sleep last night and Mr Durrant very kindly offered to put me up and——'

The girl laughed, a high, metallic laugh. 'Perrin's the name—Yvonne Perrin. I'm the girl that Harn is going to marry.' She waved her left hand and Gemma saw the emerald that flashed there. 'But there's no need to explain to me, my dear, I'm quite accustomed to his little ways. I certainly don't begrudge him his bit of fun on the side.' She eyed Gemma up and down superciliously. 'I take it he's not here?'

'He's—he's left for the office early,' Gemma said. Harn engaged—to this glittering bit of nastiness! And he had said he wasn't in the marriage market.

The sea-green eyes narrowed. 'Then you'd better hurry up and go after him, hadn't you? If you really are his secretary, that is, and not some little tart he picked up last night.'

'How dare you?' Gemma flashed out with one hand, goaded beyond all thoughts of caution. But before she could connect with that lovely, sneering face her arm was caught in a steely grip and twisted.

'Oh no, you don't try that on with me.' Gemma was flung backwards and collapsed in a heap on the floor, the towel trailing round her.

The girl stood over her and for one awful moment Gemma thought she intended to kick her in the face, but instead she leaned over and smacked her cheek hard. 'Just remember that, my girl,' she bit out viciously, 'and don't try crawling into my fiancé's bed in future!'

She turned and swept out of the room and the front door slammed behind her.

Gemma picked herself up, rubbing her cheek and seething inside with rage. She dressed rapidly, talking to herself while she did so, dragging her tights on so that they laddered, which small disaster brought her close to the tears she wouldn't shed on account of the nasty little scene that had just taken place. 'This is the end, Mr Harn

Durrant,' she vowed, as she rubbed soap on the end of the run. 'If you think I'm going to stay here to be insulted and attacked by your girlfriends, you can think again!' She would hand in her notice as soon as she reached the office, and leave for Lessington and a peaceful life at the first possible moment.

And I so nearly fell under his spell myself! She shuddered as she remembered last night. I so nearly kidded myself I was in love with the man! She wanted nothing more to do with him, she just wanted to get away quickly and never see him again.

She dragged a comb through her hair, rummaged in her bag for some powder-cream to dab on her cheek, which was still stinging, and went into the hall to find the number of a taxi firm.

Miss Wright was sitting at her desk as she went into the office. Harn was standing beside the desk and as soon as Gemma entered the room she saw that something dire had happened. She had seen him look angry before, but never *this* angry, never the blazing rage that he was so obviously controlling with the utmost difficulty.

'So here you are at last!' he snarled. 'Now come and sort this one out.'

Gemma's eyes went from the accusation on his face to the smug satisfaction on May Wright's. 'W-what's the matter?' she stammered. 'What's happened?'

'What's happened,' he said chillingly, 'is that there's no trace of my report for today's meeting. Miss Wright couldn't print it out because it's not there on the disc. Not in the index, not on the duplicate disc either. Where the blazes is it?'

Gemma's inside cramped as she remembered sickly that she hadn't duplicated the disc before she left last night. One of the first rules of using a word-processor was to duplicate any disc that you didn't intend to print out straight away. She had been in such a hurry to get to the party to help Brenda that she had forgotten to do it.

But the original document on the original disc— what had happened to that? It couldn't have just disappeared—it couldn't! Not unless someone had deliberately deleted it. She caught the gleam of triumph in May Wright's pale blue eyes, and was suddenly sure that was what had happened. It would be the work of a couple of minutes, to anyone familiar with the machine, to wipe out all trace of the report by simply calling up the index on the screen and deleting that particular document.

'Let me look.' She almost pushed Miss Wright out of the chair and sat down before the word-processor. By this time she knew her way about it blindfold; it was an old friend. She knew exactly which keys to press to bring up the wretched report on the screen. But after thirty seconds it was apparent that it just wasn't there. Report No. 46a was missing from the index and that was that.

'Well?' Harn barked.

'It's—it's not there,' she faltered.

He drew in a deep breath through his nose. 'I know it's not bloody there! What do you intend to do about it? My meeting's at twelve—it's nearly ten now. I've been working on those figures for days.'

There was no time for argument or excuses—or even for accusations against May Wright—and anyway, she couldn't prove anything. This was an emergency. Gemma's mind was suddenly ice-cold. 'I've still got the tape you dictated the report on,' she said, hoping that the horrible Miss Wright hadn't found that too, and wiped it clean. 'And I've got the first print-out, the one you did all the revision on. I think that between the two I could type out the report again in—say—an hour and a half.' She wondered if that were humanly possible, even while she said it. Well, it would jolly well have to be.

Harn was staring at her grimly. 'All right, get on with it, then. That won't give me time to check it before I leave, but I'll have to risk it.' He jerked his head towards Miss Wright. 'Off you go,' he said.

Miss Wright fluttered her hands. 'Isn't there something I could do to help, Mr Durrant? I could——'

'Out,' he said, and opened the door for her, and with a last spiteful look in Gemma's direction Miss Wright left the office.

At the end of an hour and a half, or shortly less, the report was typed. Gemma felt like a squeezed-out rag. Her head was spinning with dollars and yens and all the language of electronics with which she still wasn't quite at home. But she had done it.

She carried it in to Harn's office and laid it on the desk before him. He looked at it. 'Good,' he said briefly.

Gemma went back to her own office and sat with her head in her hands. All she wanted to do was to get away from this place, from London, from Harn Durrant. It had been a terrible mistake from the beginning. But she would wait until the

Japanese contract was finalised before she gave in
her notice. At least, she thought wryly, he would
have no difficulty in replacing her. May Wright
was fairly panting on the sidelines, waiting for the
call to launch her into the game. She'd been
determined to get the job and not at all averse to
playing dirty to do it.

This isn't my scene, Gemma thought unhappily.
I'm just a small-town girl after all. I can't compete
in the rat-race.

Harn emerged just before twelve and she got to
her feet. 'Is it—will it do?' she asked nervously,
with a glance towards his briefcase.

He looked tense and grim as he replied shortly,
'It had bloody well better do.' Then, without
another word, he went out of the office.

Five minutes later Brenda appeared. Her face
was white and drawn and she looked nothing like
her usual confident self. 'Gemma, I had to come
to—to say I'm sorry.' She stood before Gemma's
desk like a culprit before a headmistress. 'Last
night—I don't know what came over me, I guess I
must have had too much wine and I—I lost my
head completely. I said some awful things to you
and I didn't really mean them, and of course it has
nothing to do with me, what you choose to do.
Anyway——' she spread out her hands '—I'm
sorry, and that's all I can say.'

Gemma got to her feet. 'Let's forget all about
it,' she said, and saw the slow smile that appeared
on the other girl's face.

There was a silence in the small office, then
Brenda said, 'What do you say if we go out and
have some lunch at the Tavern? On me, of course.'

'I'd like that,' Gemma said simply. She picked

up her handbag, locked the office door, and they went out together. Harn wouldn't be back for some time yet and if there were any phone calls it was just too bad. She felt as if she had already resigned her responsibility here.

'You're not really serious about leaving, are you, Gemma? Why, you've only just come, and you're doing very well.'

The two girls had walked down to the river after lunching off sandwiches and lager at one of the many old pubs in the City. Gemma stood watching a heavily-laden river steamer plough its way slowly under the bridge before she replied. 'Yes, I'm really serious. I don't fit in here, Brenda, and that's the truth. I thought I was ambitious to be a top secretary and so on, but somehow I've changed my mind.'

Brenda eyed her sagely. 'Is it because of Harn Durrant? You've fallen for him, like the rest of us.'

Gemma didn't answer immediately. She stood staring out across the grey water, trying to think, trying to be honest with herself. At last she said, 'I suppose you're right, Brenda. I've been confused about the job and the people at the office—Miss Wright in particular—but yes, I suppose it's really because I'm trying to persuade myself that it would be asking for unhappiness to stay around Harn any longer. I know quite well there's no future with him for a girl like me. And by the way——' she turned to Brenda with a twisted little smile '—I encountered this Yvonne woman this morning and we had a slight—disagreement. She informed me that she was engaged to Harn and waved a great emerald ring at me.'

Brenda raised her dark eyebrows. 'Oh, she did, did she? I'd say that's wishful thinking. Harn Durrant isn't going to marry anyone, if my guess is right.' She laughed harshly. 'At least, not until he's seventy and needs a wife to warm his slippers.'

Suddenly she put a hand on Gemma's arm. 'You're right, Gemma, get away from the man before you get in too deep. He can tear you apart—and don't I know it! You may have heard on the office hot line for gossip—about me, I mean. I went over the top for him, put my marriage at risk—and ended up in hospital with an overdose. No, don't say anything, my dear——' as Gemma gave a horrified little gasp and would have spoken '——it all happened last year and it's water under the bridge now. I thought, until last night, that I was over it, but it seems that I wasn't. Look at the way I reacted when I thought you'd been sleeping with him. Pure feline jealousy, that was, I'm ashamed of myself, I can tell you. That man gets under your skin.'

'I hadn't, you know,' Gemma said quietly. But she knew that it had been touch and go, and if Brenda hadn't telephoned——

She glanced at her watch. 'I'd better get back. Thank you for being so—so frank with me, Brenda. It's helped me to make up my mind.'

Back at the office the porter said, 'There's someone to see Mr Durrant, Miss Lawson—a Mr Underhill. I've put him in the waiting room. Mr Durrant's not back yet—will you deal with it?'

'Oh yes, thank you, Grayson. I know Mr Underhill, I'll go up and see him.'

Derek was sitting at a polished table reading a

magazine. He jumped up when she opened the door and his fair face lit with pleasure. 'Gemma—I hoped I'd see you. How are you?' He took both her hands and squeezed them hard.

'All the better for seeing you, Derek.' She gave him a sunny smile. He brought with him everything that she had left behind—Lessington—and home—and the shabby old office of Durrants (Fine Paper), and all that she felt confident of measuring up to.

'The boss is out, they tell me,' he said, and she nodded.

'He may be quite a while. An important meeting.'

'Splendid! Then you'll have time for a chat.' He drew her down to a leather chesterfield that stood against the wall in the luxuriously-furnished waiting room. 'I want to hear all your news and how you're liking London and the job and everything. Is it going swimmingly?'

She looked away from his nice, concerned face, blinking back quick tears. 'Gemma! What's up?' He turned her round to face him. 'What's gone wrong?' He grinned crookedly. 'Tell Uncle Derek.'

She sniffed and blew her nose. 'Pretty well everything's gone wrong. I—I've almost decided to pack it in.'

She couldn't miss the look of hope that spread over his face. 'And come back to Lessington?'

'Where else?' she said. 'It's my home.'

He didn't speak for a full minute, just sat looking at her delightedly. 'Well, that's the best news I've heard in ages!' He flushed. 'I can't tell you how disappointed I was when you left—just when I thought we were getting to know each

other. Can we go on where we left off, Gemma?'
He leaned towards her, taking her hands.

The door burst open and Harn stood there, his
eyes on Gemma, sitting with both her hands
enclosed in Derek's. The two on the chesterfield got
to their feet, and Derek stepped forward, one hand
held out tentatively. 'I looked in to see you as I
happened to be in town, Mr Durrant.'

Harn gave Derek a long, cold look, ignoring his
outstretched hand. 'Have you anything to report?
Anything to consult me about?' he rapped out.

'Well, no, not exactly,' Derek replied awkwardly.
'Things are going along quite well in Lessington,
and——'

Harn nodded curtly. 'Good. Then, if you'll
excuse me, I have work to get on with. Come into
my office, will you, Gemma.' He turned and
walked out of the room.

Derek had turned crimson. 'Well, blow me
down—how rude can you get? I almost feel like
giving up the whole job!'

Gemma put a hand on his arm. 'Don't do that,
Derek. He's in a bad mood today, that's all.
Things have gone rather wrong.'

He grinned wryly. 'O.K., I'll take your advice.
I'm going back this evening. Keep in touch, won't
you, you know my office address. Please, Gemma.'

She gave him a smile, but no promises, and ran
back to her own office. Harn had fuelled her anger
still further by his rudeness to Derek and she had
to give him her notice and get it over with before
she could change her mind. She wondered if the
Japanese deal had fallen through and if that was
why he looked so specially grim when he walked
into the waiting room just now.

She followed him into his own office, as he had ordered her, and stood beside his desk and waited. He leaned back in his chair, stared at her for a moment in silence, then said, 'Well, aren't you going to ask me how the meeting went? As a good secretary you should be involved.'

She didn't like his ironic tone at all, but she said, 'How did it go?'

He smiled suddenly and she looked away because if he smiled at her like that her resolve might be weakened. 'Splendidly,' he said. 'It's in the bag.'

That was her cue, then. She was shaking inside, but she said quite calmly, 'I'm glad the report was all right. I'd have been sad if my swan song had turned out to be a disaster and spoiled the deal for you.'

'Swan song?' he said absently. 'What on earth are you talking about?'

She took a long deep breath. 'I'd like to give in my notice, Mr Durrant. And I'd like to leave straight away. I'm sure Miss Wright will be quite happy to fill my post.'

She really had his attention now. 'Don't be silly, Gemma, of course you can't leave just like that!' He almost barked out the words, then added more quietly, 'It's most inconvenient.'

'But I can,' she said. 'I shan't expect to be paid, of course. I don't know what the correct procedure is. Do I pay you a month's salary in lieu of notice?'

He made a noise of extreme exasperation. 'Look, this nonsense has gone far enough. I won't accept your notice, my girl, so that's that.' He jerked his chin out aggressively. 'What's the idea, Gemma? Why this sudden change of heart? I thought you were keen to learn, to get experience, to be a top secretary?'

'I thought so too at first,' she said, and was surprised how calm and reasonable her voice sounded. 'But it didn't work out, did it?'

'Oh, you mean this business of the report this morning?' A smile of relief crossed his face. 'You mustn't take that to heart. As a matter of fact it wasn't important after all. Mr Okimo had made up his mind, apparently, even before we met for lunch, and the report wasn't vital. So don't let that little slip-up worry you. And anyway——' he looked grim suddenly '—I'm not altogether convinced that it *was* your slip-up. The Wright woman was fussing about with the discs. I shouldn't be at all surprised if she messed the whole thing up before you got here. I've been doubtful about her work for some time. I think she'll have to go.'

Gemma shook her head stubbornly. 'It's me that's going.' Oh, please, *please* don't look at me like that, as if you cared, as if you minded whether I was here or not.

He slapped a hand hard on the desk. 'No, Gemma, I won't let you go, even though your grammar still leaves a lot to be desired.' He smiled, inviting her to share the joke, to give up this ridiculous idea of leaving. He was so sure he could make her change her mind.

She turned her head away, because when he smiled at her and the long dark lashes brushed his cheek she remembered how it had been when he held her in his arms last night and her insides melted and she was afraid her resolution would weaken. Then she put a hand to her cheek, where the girl Yvonne had slapped her as she lay on the floor. Yvonne, who was wearing his ring. Even if he didn't marry Yvonne, there would still be a long trail of girls wanting him. She couldn't stay here and watch that. Not after last night.

'I'm sorry,' she said, biting her lip hard. 'I'm leaving. Today.'

Harn's face hardened and she saw that at last she was getting through to him. 'Is it that young fool Underhill?' he said very nastily. 'Is that why you're so keen on letting me down?'

Gemma said nothing. Let him think what he liked. It would probably be easier if he thought she was leaving on account of Derek.

He got to his feet and glared at her across the desk. 'All right then, go,' he bit out the words icily. 'It serves me right for ever taking you on. I might have known you would let me down. I shouldn't have expected loyalty from a chit of a girl like you.' She had never seen him like this, white with anger. 'But don't come crawling back to me if you want a job again, or want me to take back that sister of yours—I've finished with the lot of you. Now get out. Get *out!*' He took a step towards her and she could feel the violence seething in him and her stomach turned over as she thought he might strike her.

She gripped the edge of the desk to steady herself. She was trembling all over and her knees felt like jelly. She had never dreamed it would be as bad as this—that he would react with such rage. She didn't stop to wonder at it. For a long, dreadful moment she stared at him, her eyes wide with alarm, and then she turned and ran out of the office.

She had left her dressing case—the one that Harn had brought her from Brenda's this morning—in the ladies' rest room, and she dived in there now, like a terrified small animal diving into its burrow. The room was empty and she closed the door and leaned against it, panting and sobbing under her breath. Any moment she expected to hear Harn banging on the door, ordering her to come out. But after a few minutes she calmed down. Of course he wouldn't come after her, why should he? He was probably congratulating himself already that she had gone, He would be telling himself that he'd been stupid to take on a young, flighty girl in the first place.

She crossed the room and stared into the mirror at her distraught face. I did it, she told herself, I got away from the danger. Sooner or later the opportunity would have arisen again and he'd have got me into his bed, and I couldn't have resisted him. None of the others could, could they, so how could I expect to? So much wiser, sometimes, to run away and never mind that silly, childish thing about never refusing a dare. This time there was no chance—not even a remote chance—of winning. She'd been sensible and she should be patting herself on the back, not weeping with this awful sense of loss. Come on, Gemma, pull yourself together. Collect your things from Brenda's flat and then get on the next train home.

Home—how good that felt! Still shivering, she swilled her face with cool water, did what she could with her make-up to repair the ravages of the last few minutes, took her dressing case from her locker and walked out to the lift, looking straight ahead of her. As she stepped out on the ground floor a man came quickly towards her across the wide lobby, his step making no sound on the rubber flooring. She recoiled. Harn had come to drag her back to vent that terrifying anger of his on her again.

But it was Derek Underhill. 'I was just plucking up courage to come back and make sure you were all right,' he explained. 'You looked so——' he laughed awkwardly '—I thought you might need rescuing.'

Gemma looked into his kind, ordinary face. 'Maybe I did,' she said slowly. 'But I got away by myself. I'm leaving, Derek. I'm on my way out. Will you take me back to Lessington with you?'

'Won't I just?' he agreed enthusiastically. 'Here, give me your case. Where are the rest of your things? I'll get a taxi and we'll collect them, O.K.? Then we can catch the six o'clock train from Paddington.'

He took her case in one hand and his other arm went round her protectively as they reached the exit. At that moment one of the lift gates clanged behind them and Gemma spun round, her heart racing. Harn Durrant stood outside the lift, looking fixedly across the lobby at her, as she stood encircled in Derek's arm. From this distance she couldn't see the expression on his face. She drew closer to Derek. 'Come on, let's get out,' she murmured, and as they passed through the entrance door she heard the lift gate close again.

She clutched Derek's arm as they made their way down the stone steps of the great building. She felt safe again—Harn Durrant had passed out of her life.

She ought to be rejoicing, she ought to be

congratulating herself on having escaped from an impossible situation. In time she would be able to do just that, she assured herself, standing beside Derek as he tried to hail a taxi. But just now she felt she would like to die.

It was dark by the time the train arrived at Lessington and the early summer night had turned chilly. Derek's car was parked at the station and he loaded Gemma's cases in and drove straight to her home.

The house, of course, was empty and unwelcoming and Gemma went round switching on fires. Then she made coffee and found a packet of biscuits and a tin of milk in the store cupboard.

Derek came down from carrying the cases upstairs to the landing. 'It's pretty cold up there,' he said, rubbing his hands before the electric fire in the living room. 'I don't like to think of you staying alone here tonight.' Gemma had explained to him about Beth being away. 'We've got a little spare room and my mother would be delighted to put you up.'

Gemma thanked him but refused tactfully. She liked Derek, but she had to be alone—to lick her wounds and make up her mind what she was going to do next. Also, the last thing she wanted to do was to commit herself to any serious relationship—and Derek seemed to be making it plain that a serious relationship was what he wanted.

Conversation flagged as they drank their coffee, and Gemma couldn't stifle her yawns. 'Sorry,' she apologised, 'I'm being very rude. It's been quite a day, one way and the other.'

Derek took the hint and departed, after making

her write down his phone number in case she found she needed help of any kind. She thanked him and stood at the door to see him off and waved as the car moved away. Then she went in and closed the door and her thoughts were immediately back in London and living again that final disastrous meeting with Harn. There was no excuse for him to vent his ill-temper on her as he had done; she supposed she *had* behaved badly in leaving like that, without giving him proper notice. But when you came to think of it she had treated him just as he had treated Beth. If he was inconvenienced it served him right, she told herself resolutely, there was no need for her to feel guilty about it. He had confessed that he never considered anyone but himself, so he didn't merit her consideration.

Oh, but he had been kind when she had stood alone and terrified in that dark street in the middle of the night. He had been wonderful then.

Thoroughly confused and miserable, Gemma felt the tears begin to gather and opened her handbag to grope for a hankie. Here, her hand encountered Beth's letter—the one Harn had brought with her clothes this morning from Brenda's flat. She had never even opened it.

It was a surprising letter. Quiet, placid Beth was suddenly bubbling and over the moon. Wonderful, marvellous news, she said, and first of all she must tell Gemma that she was *devastated* that she couldn't have been there, but she knew that Gemma wouldn't be able to get away, when she had just started in a new job, and really it would have been foolish to put it off, because they had the offer of this apartment in a wonderful old house—really ancient Naples, rather crumbling on the outside—'but, my darling Gem, the *view*! If you look between the roofs you can actually get a glimpse of the bay and it's really as blue as they say it is. And the sun and the sky, and the wonderful old buildings, and all the galleries and museums, and—oh, everything about Naples is heaven!!!'

Gemma took a deep breath, sat down by the fire, and turned over to the next page. Here, at last, all became clear. Beth had got a job in a local school, teaching English. Ian had been offered a part-time lecturing appointment in connection with one of the art galleries, taking round parties of American and English tourists. On the strength of all this, and because one of Ian's fellow-artists here knew of this apartment, they had decided to get married straight away. 'So I'm now Mrs Ian Jackson, doesn't it sound good? Oh, Gemma dear, we're so very, very happy, I can't begin to tell you, and I know you'll be glad it's turned out so well. Do write soon and tell me that you forgive me for doing things in such a hurry, and that you understand. We don't know yet what our future plans will be, but we may well decide to settle out here. Perhaps it might be a good idea to sell the house in Lessington and we could divide the spoils, as Father left it to both of us. That is, of course, if you've decided to stay in London. Let me know what you think.

'Your loving and ecstatic sister, Beth.'

'P.S. Is there *any* chance of your coming out to see us, if only for a few days? It would be so lovely to see you and show you all the wonders. Could you ask the Durrant man to advance you a spot of

salary and give you a few days off? I think he
owes me that, don't you? On the other hand I
can't really feel cross with him any longer, because
if he hadn't sacked me when he did I shouldn't be
here now. DO TRY AND COME SOON.'

Gemma read the letter through slowly twice.
Dear, kind Beth, she deserved her happiness. But
it was a shock. Up to now she had had the thought
at the back of her mind that Beth would be
coming back soon, that somehow they would be
able to go on as they had before.

You're on your own now, my girl, she said
aloud, so you'd better get on with it. She felt a
little sick and suddenly she realised she hadn't
eaten anything for hours and hours, except a
sandwich on the train. She went into the kitchen
and opened a tin of sardines, spread them on toast
and stuck the lot under the grill. Then she sat
down at the kitchen table, where she and Beth had
had so many companionable meals together, and
ate the humble food and raised her glass of ginger
beer. 'To Beth and Ian,' she said aloud. She
laughed shakily. Sardines on toast and ginger
beer—what an odd wedding celebration!

Her eyes travelled slowly round the familiar
room, seeing all the loving care that Beth had put
into making a home for them both. The cherry-red
cushion covers on the cane chairs; the curtains to
match; the hearthrug that Beth had made herself.
There was a faint film of dust over everything
now—the wooden dresser, Beth's sewing machine
in the corner, the chair-legs. It was as if the house
was already feeling itself rejected.

No reason now for getting a top job and earning
lots of money so that she could help Beth. Beth

had done without her help. No reason to keep on this house, just for herself. She would write to Beth and agree to sell it. And then what? Suddenly the urge for success had gone, there seemed no point in ambition.

No Beth. No home. No job.

No Harn——

Gemma laid her head down on the wooden table and let the tears come.

CHAPTER EIGHT

THE feeling of strangeness was almost the worst thing of all. Next day Gemma got up and dressed and made herself breakfast, and all the time it was as if someone else were doing it all and she was looking on. The time dragged. She tidied the house and washed all the clothes she had brought back with her. Then she made herself a mug of coffee and sat down at the kitchen table to try to think what to do next.

After a time she got out her building society passbook and began to do some sums. She took out the passport which Harn had instructed her to get as soon as she started to work for him. 'You never know when you might need it,' he had said. 'I go abroad a good deal and I shall want you to come with me.'

Well, she was going to need it now, she thought very wryly, but not to go with him—to get away from him. She was going to Naples—to Beth. In this wonderful city that Beth raved about, she would be able to forget Harn Durrant, and everything that had happened in the last chaotic weeks since she first stood in front of his desk and felt the impact of those strange, thickly-fringed eyes of his that could arouse her to wild transports of longing, and just as easily shrivel her up with wretchedness. He was a danger to women, but just give me time and I'll forget him, she told herself yet again. But her body didn't seem to agree. Her body clamoured for the touch of his hands, the sound of his voice, even if he was bawling her out. She shivered suddenly. Yes, she had to get away, and Beth would understand and maybe help her to get a job.

Desperately she began to plan, and when she had drunk her coffee she walked into the town and called at the travel bureau.

'Naples? Ah, that's lovely!' The girl behind the counter raised her eyes to the ceiling. 'Really romantic. We went there last year on our Italitan tour, my boy-friend and I. Don't they say "See Naples and die"?' She giggled. 'Would you want a package, or just the travel fare?'

'I'm just enquiring the cost of the single fare, please,' said Gemma, and her face fell when she was told the amount.

'Thank you very much, I'll have to work it out.'

She tried to work it out, sitting in the park near the office of Durrants (Fine Paper). This was where she had sat on that first day—the first time she had seen Harn. Only a few weeks ago, but it seemed that he had been in her life always. She pushed the thought away and went back to her building society passbook. She had enough money to pay the fare and keep herself in Italy for a week or two, she reckoned—if—and that was the sticky part—*if* she didn't repay any of the salary she had received from Harn, in lieu of the notice she hadn't worked.

The leaves rustled in the trees; the small children squealed as their mummies pushed them to and fro on the swings; the sun shone down warmly on Gemma's fair hair and too-pale cheeks. She was aware of none of this. After a time she stood up resolutely and made her way to Durrant's office.

In the shop Ted greeted her warmly, over the heads of a couple of customers. She went through to the back office, where Mrs Brown looked up from her desk with a harassed frown, which changed to a smile of pleasure as she recognised Gemma. 'Well, well, and what are *you* doing in these parts, Gemma? I thought you were busy with Mr Durrant in London.'

'I was,' said Gemma, 'but it didn't work out. It's a long story, Mrs Brown, but—well, I left yesterday.'

Mrs Brown eyed her curiously, pushing back the strands of grey hair that had wandered over her forehead. 'That was a bit sudden, wasn't it?'

Gemma nodded. 'I'm afraid it was—I just walked out.' There was a short silence and she added awkwardly, 'Things happened that—that made it impossible for me to stay a day longer.'

'H'm.' Mrs Brown looked thoughtful and Gemma wondered if she could possibly have any idea what the 'things' were. She took a breath and rushed on, '——I've really come to ask your advice. I'm still on the books here, aren't I? I mean, my salary is paid from here, and I wondered—I suppose I should forfeit a month's salary in lieu of giving notice, shouldn't I?'

Mrs Brown pursed her lips. 'Well, it all depends, of course, on why you left so suddenly. I'd have to consult Mr Durrant about that.'

'Oh, please no, don't do that,' Gemma said quickly. 'I was wondering—do you think you could let it run on for a few weeks? You see, I've just heard that Beth has got married and she's living in Naples and I so much want to go there to see them. And if I repay my month's salary I shan't have enough for the fare.'

Mrs Brown seemed to forget all about the salary. 'Beth—married! How splendid, I'm so pleased. I'm very fond of your sister, Gemma, I was worried about her when she left, and this is wonderful news.'

She had to hear all about it, and when Gemma had finished telling her she wrote down Beth's address. 'I'd like to send her a little present and tell her how delighted I am.'

Finally, Gemma brought her back to the matter of the salary. 'Oh, you mustn't bother your head about that, Gemma dear. You take it, and go out to see Beth. It'll be a nice little holiday for you.' She looked hard at Gemma's pale face. 'You look as if you need a holiday,' she added, but she didn't ask any more questions.

'I'll fix it up with Mr Durrant some time, when he comes back,' she said. 'He'll be abroad just now—he rang me yesterday to say he was off to Japan. I expect you'll know about that. I was half expecting him to come up here before this to see how the alterations are getting on.' She lifted her chin towards the floor above from whence came the sound of hammering and banging. 'It's been pandemonium here for the last few days, since the workmen started. I haven't known if I've been on my head or my heels. But it will be very nice when it's done. You won't know it next time you see it, Gemma.'

Gemma murmured something, thinking it unlikely that she would ever see it again. All this part of her life was over.

'Why don't you go up and have a peep?' Mrs Brown suggested. 'I think Mr Underhill is up there—you know him, don't you? A very nice young man.'

Gemma hesitated at the bottom of the wooden stairs. Soon—according to the plan she had seen—they would be replaced by something far more modern and hygienic, but now they were still the same old creaky stairs that she remembered from her childhood and had climbed up so many times to see Beth. Old Mr Durrant had always welcomed her and usually had an apple tucked away in a drawer for her.

Gemma sighed. No use getting nostalgic—everything was changing. She wondered if Mrs Brown was right and if Derek was up there. It would be an opportunity to tell him her plans. He had been so kind and—in the modern jargon—so supportive, that she owed him that. She climbed the stairs, and put her head round the door of the office.

What she saw gave her a pang. It was unrecognisable as the same office where she had worked with Harn. The connecting wall to the cloakroom had been knocked out; polythene sheets flapped in the breeze where the windows had once been. Some of the floorboards were up and in the depths below there was a tangle of wires

and plumbing. The ceiling had completely disappeared and there was a yawning gap right up to
the joists supporting the roof. A smell of damp
and plaster and sawdust filled the air. Derek, in his
usual cords and sweater, was talking to one of the
workmen at the far end of the area. He waved
when he saw Gemma, and called out cheerily,
'Hang on, shan't be a sec.'

The workmen were obviously packing up to go
for lunch. The three of them clumped down the
stairs as Derek came across to Gemma, beaming
all over his fair, pleasant face.

'This is a nice surprise. I was going to call round
later on and see how you were getting along. I
thought you might like to come and have a meal
with us this evening. Mother would love to meet
you.'

He looked so hopeful that Gemma's resolution
almost failed her. Was she being idiotic in running
away? Wouldn't it be far more sensible to stay and
find a job here and start a relationship with Derek
that would, she was sure now, lead to a good,
ordinary, happy future?

'Gemma?' He touched her arm and his eyes were
pleading. It was almost as if he knew this was a
crisis moment.

She shook her head slowly and sadly. 'I'm
awfully sorry, Derek, but I can't. I've decided to
leave England—I'm going to Italy, to be with my
sister. She's just got married and she wants me to
go out there.'

'For good?' His face was suddenly white.

'I don't know,' she said.

There was an awkward silence, then Derek
cleared his throat. 'I may as well come clean, my

dear. I know we haven't seen very much of each other, but I'd hoped we might perhaps make a go of it together. I—I've never met a girl like you, Gemma. I've never thought much about love before, but since that first moment——' He broke off, flushing painfully. 'You wouldn't consider staying if—if we could——'

She shook her head. 'I'm sorry, Derek. I'm really sorry, I like you so much.'

For one awful moment she thought he was going to cry. Then he grinned crookedly. 'Oh well—I tried.'

There was the sound of steps on the wooden stairs. One of the workmen forgotten his lunch, Gemma thought absently. She moved a little away from Derek, turning towards the place where the door used to be. Then she froze, as if an icy wave had suddenly washed over her.

'Harn!' She didn't know whether she had spoken his name aloud or not.

He picked his way across the gaping floor and she couldn't take her eyes off him. He looked fantastic, she thought stupidly, she had never fully realised how handsome he was, with his dark hair and his wide shoulders under their perfectly-fitting grey tailoring. And his eyes—she caught her breath as they met her own.

'Hullo, Gemma,' he said casually, a little playfully. 'Looking for a job?'

'Not really,' she mumbled idiotically. Was he going to ignore all that had happened between them yesterday? 'I—Mrs Brown said you were in Japan.'

'I shall be, very soon, but at the moment I'm here,' with that ironic twist of his mouth.

He glanced around, nodding to Derek. 'You're getting on, I see. Nice work. No snags?

'Not of any importance,' Derek said rather stiffly, and then there was a silence.

Gemma could have screamed. If she could have run out of the room and down the stairs without tripping over the holes in the floor, she would have done so. As it was she remained rooted to the spot. The ice had settled round her now, freezing her body, her mind. She could think of nothing but that Harn was standing beside her. In a minute or two he would be gone again, but for now all she could do was stand there like a tongue-tied schoolgirl.

She was aware that Derek had spoken, but she hadn't taken in his words. All she heard was Harn saying, 'No, as a matter of fact I wanted to speak to Gemma.'

'Oh.' Derek lingered a moment, looking at the two of them. Then he said in an embarrassed voice, 'Oh. Oh, I see. Well, I'll be getting along, then, if there isn't anything——'

Harn said crisply, 'No, there isn't anything.'

Derek raised his shoulders as if to fend off a blow. Then without another word he made his way across the room and down the stairs.

Gemma fixed her gaze on where the window ought to be and watched the flapping polythene. She swallowed with difficulty. 'You wanted to speak to me?' she said. 'Is it about the salary I should pay back? I've been asking Mrs Brown about it.'

'I know,' came Harn's voice behind her. 'She told me.'

She waited, not moving.

'Gemma,' he said, very low, 'turn round.'

As if she were under hypnosis she turned, keeping her eyes lowered.

'Look at me.'

She raised her eyes and was blinded by what she thought she saw in his.

'Are you going to marry that oaf Underhill?'

That brought her to her senses—partly, at least. 'Derek's not an oaf,' she said, with sudden heat. 'He's a nice man and a very good friend.'

'Are you going to marry that nice man Underhill?' Harn said patiently, and she shook her head.

'He hasn't asked me.'

'No? That was very shortsighted of him. Because now he's lost his chance.'

He was talking in riddles again. 'What on earth do you mean?' spluttered Gemma. 'It's no concern of yours who I marry or don't marry.'

'Oh, but it is,' said Harn. 'It's very much my concern.' He glanced around him. 'I want to talk to you, Gemma, but not here, where we could fall through into the shop below at any moment. Come on, let's go to some civilised spot.' He sounded at his most masterful. It was odd, therefore, that Gemma got the impression that he was expecting her to refuse.

She rallied her defences. She said, 'I'm not sure that I want to. I left London to get away from you.'

He smiled rather grimly. 'I know you did. And I've come here to find you, so that makes us quits. You see, I need you.'

Did he want her back as a secretary? Had he come all this way to persuade her because May Wright was such a disaster?

She was in no state to work that out. She
shrugged and picked her way across the gaping
holes in the floor and down the stairs. In the shop
Ted was still deep in consultation with his
customers. 'I'll be back, Ted,' Harn called across
to him, and led the way out to his car.

He drove as fast as he dared out of the town and
turned the car's nose towards the open country
and the Cotswolds. 'I'd take you back to my flat,'
he said. 'Only you might misunderstand that.' He
flicked her a glance full of meaning from under his
dark lashes. 'There's a nice quiet little pub I know
on the way to Moreton-in-Marsh. We can get a
ploughman's lunch there.'

He said no more until they were installed side by
side on a red velvet banquette in a low-ceilinged
smoke-room, all blackened beams and polished oak
and horse-brasses on the walls.

'Cosy, isn't it?' said Harn, leaning back and
quaffing his beer.

Gemma had to say something. She said, 'I
thought you didn't like old things and old places.'
She twisted the stem of her sherry glass round and
round. She still found it impossible to meet his
eyes.

'Anyone can have a change of mind,' he said.
And added quietly, 'And a change of heart.'

The smoke-room was empty except for a couple
of farmers sitting at the bar and exchanging quips
with the barmaid. Harn put down his glass and
took Gemma's hand. 'I brought you here,' he said,
'because here in public I can't very well do the
thing I'm longing to do.'

She glanced up at him then, her eyes wide.
'Which is,' he went on, 'to take you in my arms

and hug the life out of you.' His voice dropped a couple of tones. 'Oh, Gemma, if you knew what I'd been through since you walked out of the office yesterday with your pretty nose in the air!' He put out a finger and touched the tip of her nose very gently. 'It seemed that I'd made a hopeless mess of everything and you'd gone off with that oaf—correction—with that very nice young man Derek Underhill. I whisked you away to London to get you away from him in the first place, and then, just as I was plucking up my courage to tell you I was in love with you, there he was again, holding your hand, putting his skinny arm round you. I had murder in my heart yesterday when I walked into that waiting room and found the two of you!'

Here it was, then—the danger was out in the open for her to see. She could have this man if she wanted—for how long? A week—a month? And then? She would be discarded, along with the rest.

'Gemma, say something, please! Say you're a little bit in love with me. The other night I thought you were—you were so warm and soft in my arms and you responded to me, I'll swear you did. If Brenda hadn't telephoned—well——'

She nodded. 'Yes, I know. That was why I was running away.'

'From me?'

'Of course from you.' She laughed shakily. 'Any girl would be wise to run away from you. You're a dangerous man, I told you once before that you were sexy—have you forgotten?'

'I treasure that as a valued memory.' He spoke lightly, but she heard the strain in his voice as he went on, 'I tried it on you, but I had all these reservations. You were so young, I kept telling myself. But you went to my head from the first moment I saw you—you and your blue diamond eyes and that dimple in your cheek. I wanted you quite desperately, but I felt as guilty as hell for trying to get you. And I've always believed that marriage wasn't for me. I saw what happened to my parents, they were hopelessly mismatched. It seemed too much of a risk.'

Suddenly bitter, she said, 'You could get any girl you wanted without marrying them, couldn't you? That's the trouble. As I think I told you, I don't want to join the queue. Neither do I want to start an affair with another girl's fiancé.'

'What?' he shouted. Then, with a glance around, more quietly, 'What are you talking about?'

'Aren't you going to marry Yvonne?'

A look of horror crossed his face. 'Good heavens, no! Never in this world. And she knew it.'

'She came to your flat yesterday morning before I left. She brandished a whopping big emerald ring at me. She was—particularly offensive.' Gemma touched her cheek, recalling that nasty little scene. 'It was then that I decided I'd had enough of your girl-friends and it was time to get out.'

He nodded slowly. 'Yes—yes, I think I understand.' He was silent for a time. Gemma glanced up at his face and his expression was unreadable. 'What do I have to say to convince you that none of the others mattered? That you're different—different from any girl I've known before? All right, so there've been other girls; you wouldn't expect me to live like a monk in one of your sister's ancient monasteries, would you? Although——' a flicker of amusement passed over his face '—from what I've read they weren't above a few tricks either.'

Suddenly he ran his fingers through his thick dark hair. 'Oh no,' he groaned, 'I'm making a mess of this. You see, my darling Gemma, I'm crazy about you, you've got right under my skin. I think about you all the time, you get between me and my work. I want you, I need you with me.'

Gemma looked out through the window at the little garden outside. The summer flowers were coming into bloom—poppies and delphiniums and big white daisies. She was terribly aware of the man sitting so close beside her. It was taking every bit of courage she could muster not to melt against him, to feel his arm go round her. Then he would take her back to his flat and—it would all begin. It's madness, she thought, but I love him, I want him, I can't hold out against him. I don't care about all the others, I don't care what happens afterwards.

He leaned nearer and said softly, 'Cross my heart, I've never told any girl that I loved her, but I'm telling you now, Gemma. I love you, my darling. I never expected to hear myself say that, but it's quite easy, after all, when it's true. When you mean it with all your heart.' He leaned towards her and his mouth was close to her ear. 'I love you, love you, love you.'

Her senses swam at his nearness. She only had to turn her head a fraction and their lips would meet and nobody in the room would take a scrap of notice. But he was lying when he said he had never told any other girl that he loved her. What about that letter? What about his voice saying, 'Love me? I adore you.' Oh no, this certainly wasn't the first time he'd said it.

She made one last, desperate attempt. 'I can't—can't start anything now,' she said. 'I'm going abroad.'

He drew away from her a little. 'Where—abroad?' he rapped out, in his old dictatorial manner. 'What for?'

'To Italy. My sister—Beth—has just got married and I'm going to Naples to join her there.'

'Oh, a visit, is that all?' His expression relaxed. 'Well then, no problem. We'll get married too, straight away, and go out there together. Naples would be a grand place for a honeymoon. What do you say?'

Gemma went very still and it seemed as if her heart stopped beating. Her eyes turned on his face in utter astonishment. 'Marry you?' she gasped.

'Of course. What do you think I've been talking about for the last ten minutes?'

Gemma swallowed and gulped, and couldn't say a word.

'Did you think I was suggesting some temporary arrangement?' he asked, and she nodded dumbly.

Harn groaned, and glanced round the smoke-room. A party of six—three men and three women—had just come in and were settling at the next table. 'Oh lord, this a ridiculous place to choose to propose to a girl! Why was I so scrupulous and high-principled?' He took her hand and the touch sent her senses throbbing wildly. 'Let's go back to my flat and then I can ask you properly. Will you?' His cheek brushed her cheek, and the hard roughness of his skin and the clean, astringent smell of his hair, and the deep sound of his voice made her catch her breath painfully.

'Yes,' she whispered. 'Oh, yes!'

Their hotel room had a balcony that looked down over the incredible beauty of the Bay of Naples. The sun was setting as Gemma stood leaning on the stone balustrade, her eyes dreamy, her whole body filled with a pulsating joy that had taken it over from the moment, three days ago, when she had stood beside Harn in the almost-empty Wren church in a London side street, and promised to love and cherish him as long as she lived. It must have been the quietest wedding ever. Impossible to contact Beth, who had no telephone number, while Harn's mother and stepfather were in America, visiting his only other relative, a married elder sister.

They had flown out to Italy straight away and booked in at this hotel, high up on the rocky coast of Sorrento, on the tip of the bay of Naples, and Gemma was still trying to make herself believe that she wouldn't wake up and find it had all been a dream.

'Miracles *do* happen,' she said aloud now, with a deep, satisfying sigh. 'Come and look, darling.'

Behind her in the bedroom her husband was lying stretched out on the bed, hands clasped behind his head, in an attitude of pleasurable inertia. 'Harn!' she called again, and he grunted and swung his long legs off the bed. He padded up behind her on bare feet and encircled her waist from behind, flicking up her hair and burying his mouth in the hollow at the back of her neck.

She grasped his two hands and pulled them even closer around her, thrilling to their strength and warmth through the gauzy material of the white wrapper she was wearing. 'Isn't it out of this world?' Her eyes rested blissfully on the scene below and before her: the hanging gardens and tumbling terraces entwined with scarlet and white blossoms, the lemon trees that filled the warm evening air with their heady perfume; the pink and orange palaces of Naples itself rising above the harbour, beyond the point where their hotel stood. And on the horizon, their outlines mysterious against the sunset flame of purple and gold, the islands—Capri, Ischia, Procida. Tomorrow they would visit Capri, the next day Pompeii. Long sunlit blissful days, six of them left before they must move on to fly to Japan, and Harn's business appointments there.

'It's too good to be true,' she murmured, her head against Harn's bare chest. She rubbed her cheek against the dark, springing hair there. 'And yet it is true, that's the extraordinary part. Isn't life amazing? Just when you think it's folded up on you, it can open again, like a flower?'

'Um——' He pulled her closer against him, his hands moving up to cup her breasts. 'I don't feel very philosophical just now. Come to bed.'

She gave a little gasp. Just the thought was like a warm tide rising inside her, flowing through every artery and vein. But she demurred, still gazing out across the bay. 'Have you forgotten that Beth and Ian are coming to have dinner here with us?' and added, because it was true and still delightful to her, 'Isn't it splendid that Beth's so pleased with our marriage and that we can all be friends?'

Beth's eyes had widened with shock when Gemma and Harn had presented themselves at the studio flat on their first evening in Naples, and confronted her with their news. She had been at first dumbfounded, then wary, but later, when she was convinced of her sister's happiness, and when Harn's tactful and charming approach had had time to break down her defences, she had become again the warm, outgoing Beth that Gemma loved and had kissed them both and welcomed Harn to the family.

'He's super when he's not in the office, isn't he?' she had said wryly to Gemma as they made coffee, leaving Harn and Ian talking about—of all things—football, in the studio. 'I can't get over it yet, but I'm so glad for you, Gemma love. And Ian likes him, I can tell.' That clinched the matter with Beth.

Gemma said now, 'I'm so glad you got on with Ian. Did you think his pictures were good?'

'Um?' Harn murmured, and she knew he wasn't listening. He was rubbing his cheek against her hair while his hands moved over her, awakening sensations that seemed to get more overwhelming with every fresh time they made love.

She forgot all about Beth then, and as Harn's breathing became quicker and more urgent she twisted round in his arms, pressing herself softly against the length of his body with an artless acknowledgement of her need that never failed to delight him. With a groan he lifted her and carried her into the bedroom, laying her gently on the bed while he slowly turned back the flimsy wrapper.

'Oh, but you're lovely,' he murmured huskily, 'every last bit of you.' His mouth closed her eyes and trailed down over her cheek to her breast. She shuddered, moving against him with rising excitement, and her mouth found his mouth urgently, little inarticulate cries rising in her throat as their two bodies twined desperately together, skin against skin, rising at last to a fulfilment of shared ecstasy.

Afterwards, they lay quietly in each other's arms while the sun went down over the bay, and Gemma thought, 'It took this to show me that I'm not a young girl any longer, I'm a woman, I'm Harn's wife.' The thought was still new and amazing and she gloried in it. She chuckled softly, relishing the confidence it gave her.

Beside her, Harn murmured, 'What's funny?'

Because she was sure of him now, not afraid of his anger, she said, 'Do you remember that first day I came to work for you and you left a letter dictated on the tape—a love letter?'

He lifted his head and stared down at her. 'I didn't—I'm sure—What did I say?'

Unexpectedly she felt a little shy. She said, so low that he had to lean near her to hear the words, 'You said, "Love me? I adore you." She gave an odd little laugh. 'Which on your list of girl-friends was that meant for?'

For a moment he looked baffled. Then he let out a roar of laughter. 'Oh—that! Yes, I remember now. It was an advert.'

'An *advert*?'

'Well, an idea for one. I was just doodling, trying to think of a good advertising gimmick for Durrant's writing paper. Afterwards I found out that the idea had been used before, so of course I scrapped it.' His voice changed. 'No, my darling girl, in spite of the incriminating evidence you thought you found, I was telling the truth when I said I'd never before told a woman I loved her. Never until you, my beloved little wife.'

Gemma was silent. It wouldn't have mattered—

not now—but she felt a curious satisfaction in having at last had the riddle solved for her, and so very satisfactorily solved.

'You believe me, don't you?' He stroked her smooth hair back from her face, his dark eyes glittering into hers in the dusky room. 'You believe that there's never been another girl that I wanted to keep beside me—for good—that the others are just shadows in the past, where they'll remain? You believe me?'

'Oh yes,' Gemma said softly, 'I believe you.'

His head sank back on the pillow beside hers. His arms held her close.

'Love me?' he murmured against her ear and there was a smile in his deep voice. 'I adore you.'

Harlequin® Plus

A WORD ABOUT THE AUTHOR

Why is Marjorie Lewty such a romantic?

"It's all in the way you look at the world," she states. "Maybe if I hadn't been lucky enough to find love myself—in my parents, my husband, my children—I might have viewed the world with cynicism and written downbeat stories."

As it is, she loves to write about "what is surely the most important and exciting part of growing up, and that is falling in love." The happy ending is the beginning of something else, and like all beginnings, "it must hold hope and trust and promise and love if it is to fulfill itself."

Marjorie's writing career began during the Second World War, when she signed up for a course in short-story writing. Soon she was selling stories and later serials to magazines. Then she tried her hand at a novel, and as the title of her eighth Harlequin tells us, *The Rest Is Magic*.

Great old favorites...
Harlequin Classic Library

The HARLEQUIN CLASSIC LIBRARY
is offering some of the best in romance fiction—
great old classics from our early publishing lists.

Complete and mail this coupon today!

Harlequin Reader Service

In U.S.A. 2504 W. Southern Avenue
Tempe, AZ 85282

In Canada 649 Ontario Street
Stratford, Ontario N5A 6W2

Please send me the following novels from the Harlequin Classic Library. I am enclosing my check or money order for $1.50 for each novel ordered, plus 75¢ to cover postage and handling. If I order all nine titles at one time, I will receive a FREE book, *Hospital Nurse*, by Lucy Agnes Hancock.

☐ 127 **For Ever and Ever**
   Mary Burchell

☐ 128 **Dear Intruder**
   Jane Arbor

☐ 129 **Who Loves Believes**
   Elizabeth Hoy

☐ 130 **Barbary Moon**
   Kathryn Blair

☐ 131 **Magic Symphony**
   Eleanor Farnes

☐ 132 **Mountain of Dreams**
   Barbara Rowan

☐ 133 **Islands of Summer**
   Anne Weale

☐ 134 **Night of the Hurricane**
   Andrea Blake

☐ 135 **Young Bar**
   Jane Fraser

Number of novels checked @ $1.50 each =	$ _____
N.Y. and Ariz. residents add appropriate sales tax	$ _____
Postage and handling	$ _____ .75
	TOTAL $ _____

I enclose _____
(Please send check or money order. We cannot be responsible for cash sent through the mail.)

Prices subject to change without notice.

Name _____
              (Please Print)

Address _____
                              (Apt. no.)

City _____

State/Prov. _____ Zip/Postal Code _____

Offer expires June 30, 1984   31256000000

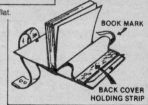

Take these

4 best-selling novels

FREE

Yes! Four sophisticated, contemporary love stories by four world-famous authors of romance FREE, as your introduction to the Harlequin Presents subscription plan. Thrill to **Anne Mather**'s passionate story BORN OUT OF LOVE, set in the Caribbean.... Travel to darkest Africa in **Violet Winspear**'s TIME OF THE TEMPTRESS....Let **Charlotte Lamb** take you to the fascinating world of London's Fleet Street in MAN'S WORLD ....Discover beautiful Greece in **Sally Wentworth**'s moving romance SAY HELLO TO YESTERDAY.

 **Harlequin Presents...** *The very finest in romance fiction*

Join the millions of avid Harlequin readers all over the world who delight in the magic of a really exciting novel. EIGHT great NEW titles published EACH MONTH! Each month you will get to know exciting, interesting, true-to-life people .... You'll be swept to distant lands you've dreamed of visiting .... Intrigue, adventure, romance, and the destiny of many lives will thrill you through each Harlequin Presents novel.

Get all the latest books before they're sold out!
As a Harlequin subscriber you actually receive your personal copies of the latest Presents novels immediately after they come off the press, so you're sure of getting all 8 each month.

Cancel your subscription whenever you wish!
You don't have to buy any minimum number of books. Whenever you decide to stop your subscription just let us know and we'll cancel all further shipments.